HONORS, AWARDS, REVIEWS given to *Jeannie, A Texas Frontier Girl, Book One*

Jeannie, A Texas Frontier Girl series is currently FEATURED CHILDREN'S BOOK OF THE YEAR at Internet Site, 2012; was BOOK OF THE MONTH and GRAND PRIZE at several Internet sites and an OUTSTANDING AUTHOR AWARD was given to Evelyn Horan by LISA'S BOOK REVIEW CAFE.

"I love every page of the book...You are a modern day Laura Ingalls Wilder...The best I have read since I picked up my first Little House Book." — J.C. Pinkerton, Content Editor, Children and Literature.

"It's always a thrill to find a book that teaches, inspires and entertains at the same time...A book for all ages...A story of love of God, country, and family." — Angie Rose, Editor, Christian Children's Books.

"A fascinating and highly enjoyable story about life in the Old West...A welcomed addition to school and community library collections." — Jim Cox, "Children's Bookwatch" Midwest Book Review.

"An exciting historical fiction with a strong sense of values." — Christina Lewis, Editor Kidsbookshelf.com.

"The time period, the dangers and perils the two friends, Jeannie and Helga face, on almost a daily basis, remind me of the Tom Sawyer and Huck Finn characters (female version)...A well-written and educational book." — John Savoy, CEO, Savoy International Motion Picture Company.

"My name is Allie and my grandmother bought me your book. I just finished reading it. It was great and my teacher was interested in it, too. Jeannie and Helga are a lot like my friend and I. — Sincerely, Allie," 3rd grade, South Carolina.

"This book was fun, interesting, and exciting! I could not put the book down." — Jessica, 5th grade, Nevada.

"Usually, I don't like western books except for *Hank the Cowdog*, but I enjoyed your book. It was cool that Jeannie could help Helga learn about ranch life. I am 12. Yours truly, Kayla," — 6th grade, Lubbock, Texas.

"I loved your Book One. I want to read Book Two! God bless you. Sincerely, Victoria," — 3rd grade, California.

REVIEWS FROM LIBRARIANS, EDITORS, CHILDREN, AUTHORS, ADULT READERS
Jeannie, A Texas Frontier Girl, Book Two

"*Jeannie, A Texas Frontier Girl, Book Two*, is wonderful! Our young girls need good books to read, and I am so thankful for an author like you who can provide them." — Faye N., Director, Gatesville Public Library, Gatesville Texas.

"An enjoyable book! I am in the process of making up an Accelerated Reader quiz for the book so students can get credit for it in our AR program." — Middle School Librarian, Texas.

"*Jeannie, A Texas Frontier Girl,* series are enjoyable and delightful books. I feel every child should read this family historical fiction. They are good books for classroom teachers to develop a teaching unit using the time period, the customs, the way of life and the emphasis on faith as a part of the tradition of America's pioneer families." — Ms. Angie, Principal, Pacific Harbor Christian School, California.

"Another Great Historical Fiction!" — Christian Lewis, Editor, Kidsbookshelf.com.

"The exciting adventures of Jeannie and her friends continue! You cannot get Jeannie out of your mind. Now that's writing!" — J.C.Pinkerton, Editor KidzLit.com.

"I can see why reviewers are likening the Jeannie series to those of Laura Ingalls Wilder's 'Little House' books. My husband and daughters are teachers, and I am going to share Book One and Book Two with them for their classrooms." — Elaine, Editor, (a teen Christian periodical).

"Evelyn Horan has done it again! She's written another heart-warming book that children and their parents will surely enjoy for years to come!" — Angie Rose, Editor, E-Christian books.com.

"My daughter, Michelle, loves the Jeannie books so much that she had me order copies of both books for the school library! The entire Jeannie series is a series even "big people" will enjoy!" — Victoria Taylor Murray – author, *The Lambert* series.

"Readers both young and old look forward to growing up with Jeannie and her friends. Young readers have a new heroine and a noteworthy role model." — Beverly J. Scott, author, *Righteous Revenge.*

"Absolutely the best for children and adults! Mrs. Horan is our present day Laura Ingalls Wilder!" — Christy French, author, *Chasing Horses.*

"My grandmother and I enjoyed your *Jeannie, A Texas Frontier Girl, Book Two.* (They are just not long enough!) Keep up the good work." — Jean & Jessica, Gatesville, Texas.

"I just finished reading Book Two. It was great and adventurous! I would like to get Book Three! I am in the fourth grade at a Christian school you visited. Love, Victoria O." — California.

I am in the third grade in Pennsylvania. I like the adventures that Jeannie has with her friends. I want to be a writer someday just like Evelyn Horan. Love, Cassidy." — 4th grade, Pennsylvania.

HONORS AND REVIEWS FOR *Jeannie, A Texas Frontier Girl, Book Three*

"Excellent historical series for children and adults." — Lisa, Editor, Bookreviewcafe.com.

"Delightful read for the child in all of us." — Christy, Reviewer, Midwestbookreview.com.

"Fun story about life on the wild Texas frontier during the 1880s." — Christina Lewis, Editor, Kidsbookshelf.com.

"This series of books is an exciting and educational experience for young readers to help them learn the customs and daily life of a different era. I eagerly anticipate Book Four!" — Kathy Bosworth, Reviewer, Denise's Pieces Book Reviews.

"Delightful read! The books remind us of the 'Little House' books by Laura I. Wilder." — Grandmother Jean and granddaughter, Jessica, Gatesville, Texas.

"Well-plotted and lively book – Excellent for gifts." — Beverly J. Rowe, Reviewer, MyShelf.com.

"Entertaining read for all ages!" — Jennifer Leese, Reviewer, A Story Weaver's Book Reviews.

"A fabulous series for children of all ages." — Victoria Murray, author, *The Lambert* series, and daughter, Michelle.

"Interesting and entertaining for readers of all ages." — Beverly J. Scott, Reviewer, Intriguing Authors and Their Books.

REVIEWS FOR *Jeannie, A Texas Frontier Girl Book Four*

"The last in the Jeannie series books will bring tears and laughter, but it will also leave the reader with a warm, comforting feeling of having visited with old friends. An outstanding series for adult and child alike, filled with characters who have become family, with plenty of warmth and love, and rounded out with enough historical information to edify while it entertains. A highly recommended series!" — Christy Tillery French, author. *Chasing Demons, The Bodyguard.*

"Jeannie, A Texas Frontier Girl, Book Four, will leave readers smiling. It's gratifying to see Book Four of the series end exactly the way the reader hopes it will – in a happy, positive conclusion. Jeannie and her best friend Helga have faced all of life's trials and tribulations, and through perseverance, along with a warm, loving friendship, and their faith in God, they have prevailed. Jeannie's horse ranch has succeeded, as has her personal life. Her future looks bright and promising, giving readers encouragement that, in their own lives, they too can overcome hardship and loss. This is a wonderfully written story that young and old alike will find endearing and entertaining. Thank you, Evelyn Horan, for the memories your Jeannie series evokes of an earlier era on the Texas frontier." — Jeanne Glidewell, author, *Soul Survivor, Leave No Stone Unturned.*

"We must say goodbye to Jeannie and her friends, but so many great things are happening in Jeannie, A Texas Frontier Girl, Book Four, that we are left with a good feeling, knowing that all will be well for them as they continue on into adulthood. There is much growing up, along with happiness and sadness, as they meet daily experiences. In Jeannie, A Texas Frontier Girl, Book Four, the characters learn to cope with life's realities, and to continue on undaunted, with a happy attitude of expectancy and joy as they look toward the future. A wonderful reading experience for both young people and adults! Jeannie, A Texas Frontier Girl, Books One through Four are a must for every young person's library! It will be given to our school library." — daughter Michelle; and Victoria Taylor Murray, author, *The Lambert* series.

"Jeannie, A Texas Frontier Girl series, Books One through Four, is a must read for all ages. It has meaning for all different ages. Children who read the Jeannie series draw from the characters' experiences and can compare them to their own experiences in a lifestyle many years beyond that of Helga and Jeannie. The young adult will look at the Jeannie series as an adventure into the past lives of characters that become friends, and they too will fashion their lives around the goodness the story delivers. The elderly will see the Jeannie series as a scrapbook, recording all the things that their children and grandchildren have done. To these older folks, it will be an everlasting memory of their lives as well. Author, Evelyn Horan, of Jeannie A Texas Frontier Girl, Books One through Four, has captured the essence of Christ's teachings and interwoven the lives of two young girls around God's golden rule. It is a lesson that can teach young and old alike. I look forward to the continuing story of Jeannie and Helga as they too, like all of us, become elderly, for the story cannot just end. It is an experience in life that must go on from one generation to the other. It is too good a story to be lost!" — Ivan Cain, author, *The Year 2012.*

"Horan has written another fascinating historical fiction novel about life in the Old West. Based on historical fact, JEANNIE, A TEXAS FRONTIER GIRL, BOOK FOUR, is set in the Eastland/Ranger, Texas area during the 1880-90s. Jeannie is a strong-willed tomboy. Once again, Jeannie and her best friend Helga find exciting adventures.
"Evelyn Horan's book flows well. The book is filled with detailed scenery. The charming characters are realistic, and the dialogue makes you feel as though you are actually taking part in their conversation – in person! She keeps the readers interest with her stimulating style of writing. Horan keeps the suspense going from chapter to chapter, leaving the reader wanting more. JEANNIE, A TEXAS FRONTIER GIRL, BOOK FOUR would make a wonderful addition to school libraries, and

public libraries, as it educates, motivates, and entertains. Educators of children ages eleven and up could easily use these books to explore the time period as well as the traditions and way of life for American pioneer families. This book is intended for young adults, but it is enjoyable for all ages. Sadly, this is the last in the Jeannie series. This reviewer looks forward to reading more books by this talented author, and highly recommends JEANNIE, A TEXAS FRONTIER GIRL, BOOK FOUR by Evelyn Horan." — Reviewer, Jennifer L.B. Leese, Maryland Author, http://www.geocities.com/ladyjiraff.

BOOK 4

JEANNIE, A TEXAS FRONTIER GIRL

By
Evelyn Horan

PublishAmerica
Baltimore

First printing

ISBN: 1-4137-3443-X
PUBLISHED BY PUBLISH AMERICA, LLLP
www.publishamerica.com
Baltimore

Printed in the United States of America

DEDICATION

Jeannie, a Texas Frontier Girl, Books 1,2,3, and 4,
Were Written For Children And Grown-Ups Everywhere,
Who Love To Read About the Texas Frontier,

Especially For My Relatives from the Schaub, Lengenfeld
and Bannert Lineage, My Pollock and Edwards Relatives,
My California Relatives, the Hollomons and Kochs, and
especially for Desarae, Patrick, Sonny, Frances, Dianne,
Richard, Mike, Virginia, Jeannie, Bill, Bob, Carl, Sal,
Jaimie, Alma, Dono, Joe, Elmer, and young folks Kade &
Baily McDaniel, Ethan Davidson, Krysta & Cherish
Hollomon, and all their family members.

For My Texas Pioneer Ancestors From Germany,
And For My Tennessee Pioneer Ancestors,
Who Migrated by Covered Wagon to Arkansas,
And On To West Texas—All, Gave Me Many Happy
Childhood Memories.

ACKNOWLEDGEMENTS

My special thanks to my Gatesville, Texas, cousin, Patsy Ruth Schaub Thompson, for colorful illustrations of Texas flora and fauna, and to Luke Smith, a Texas rancher, in Windthorst, Texas, for wonderful photographs of his longhorn cattle, horses, and animals. Thanks also to LaVerne Bevers of Archer City, Texas, for her friendship, and my grateful thanks to Editor J.C. Pinkerton, who kindly featured *Jeannie, A Texas Frontier Girl* books many times at her Internet sites, and to Ivan and Dora Cain for continuing to feature the Jeannie Book series as CHILDREN'S BOOKS OF THE YEAR at http://www.2012.freeservers.com.

My thanks to my great-aunt Era Pollock who recalls much of my father's family history in their early days in frontier Texas. She tells me, as a source of family pride a Bible was given to my great-grandmother, Fanny Pollock, by her sister's child. Her niece, Pearl Buck, the well-known writer of the twenties and thirties, wrote an inscription stating: "To my Aunt Fanny, from your loving niece, Pearl Buck."

Thank you to my daughter Alma, and to Patrick McDonnell for help and technical assistance in computer technology. Thanks to Carl McKay, for illustrations on flyers and maps of frontier Texas in the 1880s, and my thanks to the PublishAmerica staff and Pat Barto, Design Production Manager, for her lovely book cover work. My grateful appreciation to Loretta Burdette, Production Department, Miranda Prather, Executive Director, Sarah Becker, Text Production Manager and Theresa Hummer, Editorial Department for their professional time and helpful interest in the development of the *Jeannie, A Texas Frontier Girl* series. Thanks to Jeane B. Pruett, President, Central Texas Historical & Genealogical Preservation,

Inc., Museum, Ranger, Texas, for photos of historic Ranger. A special thank you to the friendly and welcoming Texas librarians in Eastland County and Coryell County for their warm acceptance of *Jeannie, A Texas Frontier Girl*, series. Finally, a thank you, to my dear friend, Jeannie Schleppe, Ranger, Texas, for her encouragement through the years and for her research into Ranger's early oil history.

A NOTE OF EXPLANATION

For the sequence of events in my narrative, I have taken many fictional liberties in locations of acreage owned by characters in my story, as well as in setting, and the use of the automobile and the discovery of oil in Ranger, Texas, by placing them in the late 1890s. However, the actual oil strike, and the common use of the automobile occurred in the first quarter of the 1900s. For further information concerning the history of Ranger, Texas, please contact Jeanne B. Pruett in Ranger, Texas. (See Acknowledgements.)

PREFACE

The Comanche Indians were nomadic, which means they had no permanent home. They moved about in search of food, generally following the buffalo from the Platte River in Nebraska to the Mexican border. During early frontier days, the Comanche roamed the grassy plains of Texas.

They were a proud and brave people. Their culture stressed the importance of being good warriors. They also counted their wealth by the number of horses they owned. A warrior was encouraged to steal whatever he could from other tribes.

As more and more settlers poured into Indian lands, buffalo became scarce. It was difficult for native Americans to survive. Many were unhappy about the changing times. Some felt it was necessary to raid settlers for food and horses, and a few tried to drive the unwanted settlers out of their hunting grounds.

After a time, Indian tribes were given reservation lands by the United States government. Today, our government is sorry about the fact that it was not more considerate of the Indians and his lands during the years of expansion. It is now trying to make up for the wrongs done to the Indians in those early days when America was young.

We admire and respect the Native American nations in our country, and we appreciate their culture and their contributions to our history. But there was a time when things were different. In Texas during the late 1800s, the Comanche Indians were still feared by many settlers.

TABLE OF CONTENTS

Chapter 1
"Building A Ranch House"

West Texas
May 1889

"Oh, my! Look how fast they are putting the roof on your house, Jeannie," Helga said, giving her best friend a hug. While standing at the new water well, the girls looked to the roof above and watched the menfolks hammering on roof boards, and placing them around a stone chimney on the east wall of the clapboard ranch house.

"Uh-huh, Jeannie said, shaking her head. "I just can't believe my new house will be ready for me to move into by tomorrow." Jeannie dipped a gourd dipper in the water bucket sitting on the circular rim of the well and offered it to Helga. After drinking the cool liquid, Helga dipped more water for Jeannie.

"Well, when Pastor Thompson mentioned to the menfolks that you could use some help last Sunday, you could expect they would all turn out to help you," Helga said confidently.

"I'm so thankful," Jeannie murmured, sipping the water. She stared ahead with a faraway look in her eyes. "Oh, grannies! Give me a little pinch, Helga. After all these years of hoping and planning—at last—I can begin to think of having my very own horse ranch."

"Ja, (yes), but I knew you'd get it someday," Helga said, smiling. "You are just that determined, once you set your mind on doing something. Let's sit under that oak tree. I see some empty cane-bottomed chairs." Helga took Jeannie by the arm and strolled with her toward the oak tree.

"Helga," Jeannie said, "sometimes I used to wonder whether your Pa would sell me this land, especially when his friend, Mr. Belton, from Eastland wanted it."

"Well, your poppa and my poppa are good friends, too," Helga reminded. "They also have adjoining ranches, and my poppa knew you'd be a good neighbor." Helga smoothed her taffy-colored hair away from her face. She paused a moment lost in thought. "You know, Jeannie, it's hard for me to think about not being in school anymore as a student."

"Yes, ma'am," Jeannie said, sighing. "I reckon graduating from school two years ago was a sure sign we'd grown up."

Jeannie leaned the back of her chair against the trunk of the old oak tree and watched a yellow Monarch butterfly settle on a cluster of bluebonnets growing wild in the spring grass. For a moment, her eyes held a faraway look. "Sometimes I think about these last few years, since you and your ma came from Germany, after she saw Mr. Markham's ad in the paper saying he wanted a house-keeper for his ranch."

Helga nodded and said, "Ja, when my poppa died, Mutter (Mother) thought it would be a good idea for us to come to America and start a new life. And so, we did." Helga turned and gave her friend a questioning look. "You know what I like to think about?"

"No, what?" Jeannie asked, gazing back at Helga.

"I like to think about our last year in school. So much happened that year. Do you remember when Little Fawn taught us how to weave Comanche Indian baskets, and then Gray Wolf, her little son, took your hound dog Junior and my dog Lady, Junior's mutter, and his sister

Cutie-Pie to go hunting? Gray Wolf had such a worried look on his face when they all came running back."

Jeannie smiled, remembering. "Well, Gray Wolf was afraid he'd killed Junior with the arrow he shot at the rabbit," she said. "He missed the rabbit and hit Junior in his foot. But Little Fawn's Indian medicine, sure enough, fixed Junior's foot. In no time at all, he was up running around again and acting a little ornery, just like his pa, Ole Blue, my childhood pet. I sure do miss Ole Blue." Jeannie gave a soft sigh.

"Ja, he was a good dog," Helga said. "And he was brave too. He saved us from a rattlesnake when you and I were riding our horses near the Leon River."

"Yep, then later on, that very same rattler killed Ole Blue." Jeannie sighed again. "But after their bad fight, even when he was snake-bit, Ole Blue managed to kill that mean rattler." There was pride in Jeannie's voice.

"And now we have Ole Blue's children. You have Junior and Princess, and Billy Joe has Hunter, and there is Lady and Cutie Pie with me," Helga said, trying to sound cheerful.

"It does help to have Ole Blue's children," Jeannie agreed.

"And I have Morning Star, the son of your stallion, Diamond. I ride Morning Star, now that his mutter, Susie, is getting older." Helga chuckled, and said, "Diamond and his son can run like the wind."

"They sure can," Jeannie agreed, still lost in thought.

After a few moments, Helga's brow wrinkled into a frown. "Do you remember when we taught Gray Wolf and his little sister Prairie Flower the alphabet and got them all ready for school? And then, Vernon Wilson and his brother Eli and his twin sisters, Ruby and Pearl, were unkind to the children? I was so angry with them."

"So was I," Jeannie said with a stern look in her eyes, "but Mrs. Thompson had a talk with Vernon, and then he told his brother and sisters to be friendly with the Indian children."

"Good thing, too," Helga said. "Poppa says Eagle Feather is a wonderful ranch hand, and his wife Little Fawn has been a great help to Mutter. She helped her when she gave birth to my little three-year-old brother, Frankie. Little Fawn and Mutter are good friends."

Jeannie smiled, remembering another time. "I was really happy when Little Fawn gave me the Indian doeskin dress that she made especially for my birthday. Gray Wolf said he tanned the deer hide, and Prairie Flower said she sewed on the beads."

"I love to see you wear that dress. You look pretty in it." Helga reached over and gave Jeannie a hug. "Remember when you wore it to the Fourth of July party to celebrate my mutter and Poppa Markham's wedding anniversary—and it was also my birthday? Then Mr. and Mrs. Decker were so upset to see you wearing the dress, because their little son had been tortured and killed by Comanche Indians, even though that sad thing happened many years ago."

Jeannie pushed a strand of yellow hair away from her face and tucked it in the bun at the nape of her neck. "Yes, and your pa mentioned how Mr. Wilson had been wounded in the leg by an Apache arrow when he was soldiering at Fort Apache," Jeannie replied. "And he said Eagle Feather had lost all his relatives in the Indian wars.

And then, my pa said we all had grievances from the past, but we should all try to get along now."

"Ja, and that's what we're all doing. I'm glad about that," Helga said.

"I like wearing my dress for special times," Jeannie continued. "I remember it was after the party on that very same day that Slim, your pa's ranch foreman, rode over to the house and gave me a beautiful saddle for Diamond."

"I think Diamond likes that saddle," Helga said, smiling again.

Jeannie nodded. "I'm sure he will be a good stud for my ranch. You know how he loves to run. And he has lots of energy. He got me away from that mountain lion in a big hurry the day after we had that terrible cyclone a few years ago."

"Ja. Then your pa and my poppa went after the mountain lion and killed it." There was a tone of sadness in Helga's voice.

"I know," Jeannie said, looking at her friend's solemn face. "But they had to do it, Helga. He was a mean one, and it's possible he could have hurt someone or some other critter." Jeannie rushed on with another memory. "I can't forget how scared I was when Pa was bit by a snake in our barn, and Henry and Ma worked fast to get rid of the poison in his arm."

"Ja, and what about the time Slim was gored by that longhorn cow when he and Poppa and the cowboys were branding the little calves?" Helga shuddered and said, "That was a real scare for me."

"Oh, grannies! Me, too!" Jeannie exclaimed. "It was your ma and Little Fawn who doctored Slim's ribs and helped him heal up. I was very afraid for awhile that we would lose him, and I was also worried, because he was supposed to be my ranch foreman someday."

"He's good and strong again now," Helga said, looking to the house. "I can see him up there on the roof, hammering away on those boards."

"Yep, Slim, sure enough, is a good worker. I think he'll be a good ranch foreman. I just hope your pa doesn't mind him coming to work for me." Jeannie turned anxious eyes to her friend.

"No, Poppa doesn't mind," Helga reassured. "Eagle Feather will take over from Slim, and Waco will give him a hand with Poppa's ranch work."

"I'm mighty glad about that," Jeannie said with relief. "And I'm real happy that you've almost finished your education to be a licensed schoolteacher. I know you'll be a good one."

"Thank you, Jeannie." Helga gave her friend's arm a gentle squeeze. "I'm looking forward to taking over for Pastor Thompson. He and Mrs. Thompson are very busy ministering to the needs of so many new folks moving in and around Shinoaks and out here in the country, too." Helga shrugged and went on, "They just don't have time to teach school anymore."

Jeannie glimpsed a small fuzzy-tailed squirrel scurrying around in the branches of her live oak tree and smiled. She loved all little critters. Then she turned to Helga and looked her friend straight in the eyes and whispered in a teasing voice, "I think the best part of all these memories is that you and Billy Joe are half-way engaged; now, isn't that true, Helga?"

Helga's face colored a bright red. She bit her lower lip nervously and murmured, "Yes—but it's still a little secret. We haven't announced it to anyone yet."

"Oh, grannies! I'll keep your secret, Helga," Jeannie said, grinning. She gave Helga a warm hug. "I won't tell. After all, we ARE best friends."

"Ja, always, we will be best friends," Helga said, smiling again.

Chapter 2
"Putting the House in Order"

"Jeannie, dear, I'm going to arrange these staples and jars of canned vegetables from my garden right here on these pantry shelves," Ma said, reaching to place the items on the shelves.

"Thanks, Ma," Jeannie said, as she finished putting dishes in her kitchen cabinet. "Whew! Let's sit down Ma and have a cup of coffee and a piece of your delicious blackberry cobbler. I'm tired." Jeannie took plates, cups, and the coffeepot to the table. She brushed past Pa who had just finished putting cane-bottomed chairs around the little kitchen table.

Quickly, Pa reached over and gave her long, yellow braid a little yank. Then he grinned mischievously. "I'm mighty glad you're wearing your hair in a braid today," he said, sitting down. "I shore do love to yank on it."

"Well, I've been too busy all this month to coil it around the back of my neck. But I expect, I'll do it tomorrow morning," Jeannie said, grinning; and with a pert little toss of her head, she sat down in a new chair beside Pa and poured him a cup of coffee.

"I sure do thank you for making these cane-bottomed chairs for me," she said, reaching over and giving him a hug and a peck on his cheek. "They are very nice. And the table is pretty, too, Pa. You do mighty good work!"

Fondly, Pa rubbed his black chin whiskers against Jeannie's cheek. "I can't believe you're already seventeen going on eighteen, and now you have your own place." Pa shook his head. "It took us men all month to get everything done. It's the first of June tomorrow, and I reckon, we can say we're done all the necessary things." Pa glanced about the kitchen with a satisfied smile.

Jeannie poured cream in her coffee and turned her eyes to Pa. "I sure appreciate it. I'm beholding to everyone," she said gratefully. "And especially, to you and Ma. I know if it hadn't been for Ma and you giving me some of her inheritance money to buy this land from Mr. Markham, why, I wouldn't have my wonderful horse ranch!" Jeannie paused a moment. "And I don't think Henry and his wife, Linda Mae, would be prospering on that nice piece of land y'all gave him, if it hadn't been for some of Ma's inheritance money to help him get started."

"Well, dear, we were glad to help you both," Ma said, carrying the cobbler pie to the table. She sat across from Pa and Jeannie and cut each of them a piece of pie. Then she cut one for herself and waited as Jeannie poured her a cup of coffee.

"Since I was my niece's only living relative, she was kind enough to remember me in her will," Ma said. "You'll remember, I was as shocked as anyone else when I received that letter in the mail asking me to come to Houston to settle her estate."

Jeannie nodded and brushed a pesky fly away from her face. She took several forks and spoons from the glass jar in the middle of the table and gave her parents a set and kept one for herself. "Henry and I missed you and Pa when you were gone. I know I said it was just a 'bird's nest on the ground' to take care of the home place until y'all returned, but I really was not that confident," she confessed.

Ma reached across the table and patted Jeannie's hand. "You both did a fine job," she said. "The house was neat and clean. You surprised me by washing and ironing the kitchen curtains too. It's not easy to iron clothes and other things with that heavy black iron that you have to continue heating on the stove to keep it hot. It cools off in a hurry. I hope someday, someone finds a better way to make an iron, so that ironing clothes will become an easier task."

Ma sighed and looked at Jeannie's little stove thoughtfully and took a small bite of pie. "Dear, I hope someday, you can have a nice, new, modern stove like mine," she said. "But for now, that little stove will do its work for you."

"Soon as I finish eating this tasty cobbler pie and drinking my coffee," Pa said, with a loving wink at Ma, "I'll go out back and chop up some fire-wood for that little stove of yours, Jeannie. You'll need a good supply of it. As time passes, I reckon you'll get some good help with your wood chopping chores from Slim and Vernon Wilson, his young helper. I think you said Vernon went to school with you."

Jeannie nodded and said, "Oh, I reckon, I can swing an ax and chop my own wood, if I have to."

"I reckon, you can at that," Pa said grinning. "You can do most anything you set your mind to doing. I've had plenty of proof of that from the past."

Jeannie smiled and shrugged, "Well, I will admit, I'm a little scared about getting the ranch started up. I'll need all the advice and help I can get."

"That's what we're here for, Punkin," Pa said, using his favorite pet name for Jeannie. There was fondness in his gaze.

"Moving into a house and getting it set up for living takes lots of hard work and plenty of time," Ma said, glancing about the room. "After the menfolks from the church finished work on your house last month, it did my heart good to see how our friends and neighbors brought you these useful house-warming presents."

"Yes, they've all beem so nice to me," Jeannie said gratefully. "Mr. and Mrs. Markham gave me that hand-made quilt on my bed. I love the little Dutch girl pattern."

"It's pretty," Ma said. "I like that pattern, too."

"And Helga gave me the embroidered tablecloth she made. I remember when she was sewing on it—over a year ago, but I didn't know she was going to give it to me." There was a happy glow in Jeannie's eyes. "And Little Fawn brought me several hand-woven baskets. People have all been so thoughtful. I don't think I can ever thank them enough. I love my little house and everything in it. It's so cozy and comfortable." She gazed about her kitchen with a happy smile. "I'm expecting Prairie Flower and Gray Wolf to help me plant my garden today. I think they'll be riding over on Mr. Markham's Susie," she said, and then shook her head. "It's hard to believe that such a gentle mare is the mother of Diamond's son, Morning Star."

"She's a gentle mare all right," Pa said, rising. He reached for his straw hat hanging on the back of his chair. "But that Morning Star and Diamond are two peas in a pod!"

"They are that, for sure," Jeannie agreed. "Helga and I love to go riding. Both those horses like to run lickety-split."

"Just be careful, dear," Ma cautioned, gently stirring her coffee with her spoon. "You're a young woman now with responsibilities."

"I know, Ma," Jeannie said. "I'll ride carefully and not take any chances."

"Well, I'm going to the barn for an ax, so I can start chopping up some firewood. Just one last thing I want to say. Us men folks put up a mighty nice barn for you, Punkin. I wish mine was as new and nice as yours." Pausing at the back door with a twinkle in his eyes, Pa said, "I just hope a cyclone won't come up this winter and blow your barn away."

"Grannies, Pa! Don't even think such a thing!" Jeannie scolded. "I remember Mr. Markham lost his barn a few years back from a mighty bad twister."

"Sorry, Punkin," Pa said, opening the screened door, "just teasing. I'll be outside if you need me. Whoops! Here comes, Junior!" Pa stood aside, and Junior raced past him and came to a skidding halt beside Jeannie.

"Well, I declare, Junior!" Jeannie exclaimed. "What is that smell? Have you been chasing after a skunk?" Jeannie jumped up. "Come on, young fellar—outside you go!" She shooed Junior out the back door and closed it.

Ma chuckled. "He is quite a handful," she said, carrying her cup to the kitchen sink. "Just like his pa, Ole Blue, always into something." She pumped on the pump handle and brought in some cold water in the dishpan. "I'm so glad Pa put in a sink and a water pump for you. It sure is a big help. I remember the day he put mine in last year. What a joy!"

"I'm glad too, Ma," Jeannie said, joining her mother at the sink. "It's hard to have to carry a bucket of water from the windmill or the well every time I need water. I really feel lucky to have both a windmill and a watering trough for horses and stock."

Ma patted Jeannie's arm. "I believe Pa and you have thought of everything you might need to get settled in your own place," she said, lifting a teakettle of hot water from the kitchen stove.

At the sink she poured hot water into a dishpan and a rinsing pan. Then she reached for a bar of homemade soap from a saucer on the sink and made swishing suds with her hands in the dishpan's hot water. Then she began washing dishes and putting them in the rinse water pan.

Jeannie lifted a tea towel from the kitchen cabinet hook and dried a cup. "The one big thing I have to do soon is buy horses," she said, putting the cup in the cabinet.

"Jeannie! Jeannie!" It was Gray Wolf calling from the front of the house. Jeannie hurried to the porch steps and stood near the swing. She watched Gray Wolf tie Susie's reins to the hitching rail. Then he reached up and helped his sister dismount from Susie's back.

"Hello, Gray Wolf. Howdy, Prairie Flower," Jeannie said, turning to the door. "How are y'all, this morning?"

"We're fine," Prairie Flower said, smiling. Her large black eyes shone with excitement as she climbed the flat-stone porch steps. "We came to help you plant your garden."

Jeannie returned a friendly smile. "Well, that's mighty nice of y'all. I can use your help," she said, holding the screen door open. "Come on in the house and have a piece of berry cobbler pie and a glass of buttermilk, and then, we'll get started."

Later that night before going to bed, Jeannie looked out her bedroom window into the star-filled sky. The full moon shone brightly. She remembered Pa telling stories of how Comanche Indian warriors had often ridden down into Mexico on raiding parties when the fall October moon was full and shining so bright you could see almost as good as when it was daytime. That's when folks feared the Comanches the most. Pa said the Comanche war trail had its beginning near Amarillo around the Palo Duro Canyon area. The trail passed in this part of the country near Abilene on its way south, but the raids happened long ago, and now, Comanches were no longer to be feared.

In fact, everyone knew she was a good friend to a special Comanche couple, Eagle Feather and Little Fawn. Their children Gray Wolf and Prairie Flower had worked hard to help her plant her garden today. They were wonderful children, and she loved them dearly.

Jeannie knew Diamond was in the new barn in his stall feasting on a good portion of oats. Ma had given her some chickens, and they were roosting in their chicken coop, settled in for the night. The milk cow Pa had given her was probably lying under an oak tree in a small fenced-in enclosure near the barn. She planned to fence in a larger pasture for the cow and the baby colts that would be born on her ranch someday. Jeannie sighed. There was still a lot to do before her ranch would be ready.

She looked past the barn to the bunkhouse built on a raised knoll between several live oaks. She could see the glimmer of the kerosene lamplight shining through the bunkhouse window. Slim and Vernon must be awake. Slim was probably thinking about tomorrow's chores, just as she was.

Well, she'd fix the boys breakfast in the morning, and then Slim and she would ride into the hills. She'd been anxious to take a good look at her source of water and study out the best grassland for grazing her horses.

Jeannie turned and blew out her kerosene lamp. She was tired but happy. "Thank You, God," she murmured, drawing her quilt up close. "Thank You, Lord, for all my blessings, and thank You for giving me my wonderful, new horse ranch."

Chapter 3
"Making Plans and Visiting the Water Source"

"Cock-a-doodle-doo!"

The colorful red rooster that Ma had brought along with a new flock of hens for Jeannie's use, perched on the fence rail of the chicken coop and again crowed loudly, "Cock-a-doodle-doo!"

Jeannie opened her eyes and stretched and yawned. Outside her window, the morning sun was an orange-red glow in the sky. It was going to be a warm day for sure, and she had overslept! Slim and Vernon were probably hungry as two grizzly bears!

Hurriedly, she pulled on her overalls, brushed her hair, and put it in a long braid. When she entered the kitchen, she felt its pleasant warmth. Jeannie sighed happily. Slim had already put kindling in the stove and started a fire. Now, that was mighty thoughtful of him, but he was nowhere in sight. She supposed he was down at the barn this morning, saddling up Miss Sunrise and Diamond, getting them ready to carry the two of them on their ride into the hills. She wanted to get a good look at her source of water and see for herself how well it was running this hot June month.

Jeannie quickly mixed a batter of pancakes and put some bacon in a skillet to fry. She brought eggs from the cooler and boiled a pot of coffee. Then she poured pancake batter into another skillet and set the table for three.

"Morning, Miss Jeannie," Vernon said from the back porch doorway. "I brought a bucket of milk for you."

"Come in, Vernon. Just put it on the cabinet shelf."

"Buttercup had a mighty full udder this morning," Vernon said, setting the bucket down. "Looks like there's lots of cream in her milk."

Jeannie smiled and said, "Good, I'll churn up some butter for us—soon as I get a chance."

"Morning, Little Lady," Slim said, removing his hat and stepping into the kitchen. He brushed his fingers through his sandy-colored hair.

"Morning, Slim," Jeannie said from the stove. "Y'all sit down, and I'll bring you some pancakes and eggs. Much obliged for starting up my stove fire."

"Glad to help out," he said, sitting down at the wood table Pa had made. Vernon pulled out a new cane-bottomed chair and sat beside him.

At the stove, Jeannie filled three plates with flapjacks and eggs, and carried them to the table. "Dig in, boys," she said, sitting down. She reached for the pitcher and poured buttermilk into three tall glasses.

"Ma'am, you sure are a good cook," Vernon said, licking a drop of syrup with his tongue from the side of his mouth. "These pancakes are tasty."

"Why, many thanks, Vernon," Jeannie said. "I guess I'll get lots of practice cooking, now that I have my own place." With a merry twinkle in her eyes, she added, "And since I have two hungry cowboys to feed, I'll probably be kept plenty busy."

"Reckon, that's a fact," Slim agreed, grinning. "This good grub fills an empty hole in a man's stomach, all right."

After breakfast Slim and Vernon walked to the barn while Jeannie cleaned up the kitchen. Slim assigned Vernon the task of digging fence postholes for the cedar fence that would soon enclose the new barn corral. Holding Diamond's reins, he mounted his horse, Miss Sunrise, and led Diamond to the front porch where Jeannie waited in the swing.

After Jeannie mounted Diamond, she and Slim guided their horses past the back of the house and headed north toward the distant hills. "Slim, I wonder how much water is up there this time of the year?" Jeannie said.

"Well, I reckon there's a fair amount." Slim pushed his hat back and rubbed his forehead thoughtfully. "We've had some good winter rains, so I think there'll be plenty for the stock you're planning to buy soon."

Jeannie smiled and nodded. Suddenly she looked down at her pet and shouted, "Stay away from Miss Sunrise's hooves, Junior! She's not used to a dog following so closely."

Trotting along beside them, happily waving his tail in the air with his long, floppy ears drooping low, Junior looked first at Jeannie and then at Slim.

"Go on ahead of us. Run, boy," Slim said, motioning forward with his free hand.

At that moment, Junior pricked up his ears. He was watching a long, green lizard lying on a flat stone ahead. Still staring at the stone, Junior trotted toward it at a quick pace.

With a lighthearted laugh, Jeannie said, "He sees that big lizard. Now, if a jackrabbit were in front of us, Junior would be off like a shot out of a cannon! He loves to chase rabbits."

"Well, he'll get plenty of practice. There are lots of them around here. Anywhere the land isn't cultivated with crops, you'll find quite a few different kinds of critters,"

Slim said. "I've already seen deer up in the hills, and I heard a coyote howling the other night when I was sleeping in the bunkhouse."

"I know for sure, there's a polecat in the vicinity," Jeannie said. "Junior came in the kitchen a few weeks ago and smelled up the whole house with its stink." She drew Diamond in closer to Miss Sunrise. "We saw a mountain lion once on my pa's place, didn't we, Diamond?" Jeannie patted her stallion's neck affectionately. "We got away fast from that lion, but I really don't want to see another one any time soon." Jeannie shook her head adamantly, remembering her close call with danger.

"I sure hope you don't see one either," Slim said. "I hear tell, bears have been seen in the back woods in these parts, but those sightings were some years ago. I wouldn't want to meet up with one of them, myself." Slim smiled and gently swatted a honeybee away from his face with his gloved hand.

"My Pa said a momma bear is the worst kind," Jeannie said, watching the bee settle on a tall yellow sunflower. "Pa told me to never touch a little bear if I ever saw one. He said its ma wouldn't be far away, and she'd fight to kill, thinking I was trying to harm her baby."

"Uh-huh, I've heard that too," Slim said as their mounts began to climb the rolling hills.

They rode past thickets of brush, live oaks, and small cedars. Jeannie noticed the grass was greener as they rode deeper and higher into the hills. Here and there, she saw a tall cedar tree in the distance. She breathed in deeply. It seemed to her that all this beauty and fresh air must be what heaven was like. She felt relaxed and at peace. "Slim, I'm so happy, I could bust!" she exclaimed, unable to contain herself.

"Yep, I reckon so." Slim said, grinning. He reached out and grasped a tiny twig. With a quick twist, he broke it off from the cedar limb and plopped it in his mouth. "A cedar toothpick gives your mouth a sweet taste," he explained.

They rode silently, each enjoying the quiet beauty of the hills and soon approached the main creek, slowly winding its way in and out among the trees. "Now, we'll follow the creek," Slim said, turning in his saddle to face Jeannie. "It winds around a lot, but you can see how it widens and narrows here and there. It's coming down from a little valley between those two hills up yonder." He pointed ahead.

Jeannie's eyes followed Slim's arm.

"Best if you ride behind me now. It's a little narrow among these trees," he said, leading the way.

Jeannie nodded and followed. She could see water in the creek, running clear and flowing southeast at a steady rate. She felt relieved. Slim was right. No need to worry about not having enough water.

After skirting around cedars and oaks, their horses broke through the trees, and there, about a hundred yards ahead, she saw the beautiful source of her water. Tumbling over granite rocks from a drop of about twenty feet, a good-sized waterfall emptied into a round pool of crystal clear water that narrowed down into the creek they'd been following.

She knew the creek flowed downhill into her pasture. Then it forked into two branches; one flowed to Mr. Markham's ranch and another flowed to the land belonging to Pa and Henry. The water eventually emptied into the Leon River where she and her friends had swum through the years and fished for catfish. Those had been happy days.

"Every time we ride up here, it takes my breath away, Slim," Jeannie said, dismounting. "It's the most beautiful sight I've ever seen. It's hard to believe, it's all mine," she murmured wide-eyed.

"It's mighty pretty, all right," he agreed, taking the reins of both horses. He led them to the grassy area beside the pool of water. He dropped the reins and let the animals graze.

"Seeing all this fresh water, makes me thirsty," Jeannie said, kneeling at the water's edge. She dipped her hands into the cool water and drank. Slim slapped his hat against his knees for a moment to clear it of dust and then knelt beside her and scooped up a handful of water and drank deeply.

"That waterfall can drop heavy and loud after a big rain," Slim said as they both sank back on the grass. "Right now, it's falling kind of lazy-like, 'cause it's summertime."

"I'd love to see the waterfall after a rain," Jeannie said, gazing at the waterfall surrounded by shrubs and small cedars. "It smells so good up here. Can you smell the cedars?"

"Yep," Slim said. "It's a good forest smell up here. And the air is about as fresh and clear as it gets."

"When I buy my horses, they'll have all this wide-open space to go roaming around in," Jeannie said.

"And the good part is that the land is all fenced off, so you don't have to worry about them wandering away," Slim said. "Mr. Markham had us boys fence off this land years ago, so you're lucky that you don't have to put up any fences."

Jeannie lay back on the lush grass and watched the sun's rays peeking in through the branches of the nearby oaks. Slim stretched out beside her and shifted his hat down over his forehead. "A feller could sure sleep good up here," he said. "I hope, I don't fall asleep."

Junior poked his nose in Slim's free hand until Slim began ruffling and smoothing the hound dog's coat. Junior yawned and sighed and closed his eyes.

In a few minutes, Jeannie shifted to her side. Glancing over, she saw that both Slim and Junior were asleep. And both were snoring lightly. Jeannie grinned and stretched out again enjoying this wonderful moment at the pool beside her beautiful waterfall. Then a mischievous thought crossed her mind. First chance she got, she was going to tease Slim about being a lazy ranch foreman and falling asleep on the job.

Chapter 4
"Money for Horses"

"Thanks again for the loan, Billy Joe," Jeannie said, sitting across from Billy Joe at his desk in the bank. "I hope you know, Pa and I are good for it."

"Of course, I know you are," Billy Joe said with a friendly nod. "Mr. Davidson isn't worried about it either, and since your Pa will co-sign the note, the money will be advanced to you."

"Well, like I said earlier this morning, you know I have a sizeable savings here in Shinoaks in Mr. Davidson's bank, but I don't want to use it all," Jeannie explained, watching Billy Joe prepare the loan papers. "That's why I decided to take out a loan against my ranch."

"Mr. Davidson understands and agrees whole-heartedly with your decision." Billy Joe handed the papers to Jeannie. Then he dipped a quill feather pen into an inkwell on his desk and gave it to her. "If you'll just sign this note, one copy for the bank and one for you; and then, your pa can sign after you where it says co-signer, we'll process your loan right away," Billy Joe said in a business-like voice.

"Thank you," Jeannie said, taking the pen and signing her name at the bottom of the papers. She gave the pen to Pa sitting beside her, and he scratched his signature beneath hers.

Then Jeannie reached across the desk and gave the papers to Billy Joe. He took them, gave a copy to Jeannie, and put the other in his desk drawer. Smiling, he shook hands with her and then with Pa. "Reckon, y'all will be heading out to the stockyards in Eastland soon," he said, rising.

"Yep, we're planning to go to the auction today and look at some of the stock," Jeannie said. "I'm anxious to buy some mares for the ranch."

"I see," Billy Joe said, wrapping his fingers around his suit lapels.

"I'm going with her," Pa said with a twinkle in his eyes. "I want to make sure no smooth-talking horse trader takes advantage of my Punkin." He chuckled and gave Jeannie a little hug and stood beside Billy Joe.

"Good idea. She's a pretty independent young woman as I remember from our school days together," Billy Joe said with a teasing glint in his eyes, "although, I reckon, she can use a little of your help now and then."

Grinning, Jeannie nodded and rose from her chair. "Yes sir, I am independent, but today, I'm glad for Pa's advice." Jeannie gave Pa's shoulder a little tap.

"Jeannie, all joshing aside," Billy Joe said, giving her a friendly hug, "I sincerely wish you lots of luck with your ranch."

"Thanks, Billy Joe. When you come to visit Helga, y'all both be sure to stop by and see me."

"We'll do it," Billy Joe said. "I'll open the safe and get the money for you."

"I'd like to deposit half in my account, and I'll take the other half in cash," Jeannie said, waiting as Billy Joe turned the combination lock to the box-like, black, metal safe against the room's side wall.

In the late afternoon, returning home from the stock auction, Jeannie turned in the wagon seat to check on the string of horses tied to the back end of the wagon. They were following behind at a contented pace.

"Oh, Pa," she said. "I'm so happy. These mares and my Diamond, will help me start my remuda."

"They're a good string of horses," Pa said holding the mules' reins firmly as he guided them over the graveled, dry creek bed stretching across the dirt road. "They should give you some sturdy colts."

"I'd like to breed some cow ponies and some piebald mustangs," Jeannie said, watching a black hawk soaring against the western sky. "I love my new pinto mare. And my Tennessee Walking Horse will be useful for breeding comfortable riding horses for older folks. I hear they have wonderful, good manners. And those fast, little mustangs will work well with cattle, too."

"You have a variety of animals, all right," Pa said as the wagon bumped along past dusty brush and clumps of wild grass. "You can breed just about any kind of horse you want."

"I'm glad the barn corral and the small pasture are all fenced in. Vernon and his brother Eli gave Slim a helping hand," Jeannie continued on. "They all worked from sunup to sundown this past month to get it done."

"Yore little ranch has shore taken shape in no time at all," Pa said, giving the mules' reins a little shake. "Ho there, Bessie. Jake, step up!" he called. He turned to Jeannie and asked, "Are you happy, Punkin?"

Jeannie nodded. "Oh, Pa, I still can't believe my dream is coming true, right before my eyes. I love my ranch, and now with my beautiful horses to graze on that nice grassland, I couldn't ask for more." She shook her head and murmured, "I thank God every night, for how good He's been to me."

"He's a good God. He's shore blessed our family," Pa said. "Henry and Linda Mae's farm is thriving, and that little grandson of mine is a real humdinger!" Pa chuckled to himself.

"I'll have everyone over to dinner, as soon as I can," Jeannie promised, gazing ahead at the oaks in the distance. "I love little Matthew, too. He looks just like you, Pa. But then, so does his pa, Henry," Jeannie said.

"Well, I feel sorry for both of them," Pa said, winking at Jeannie. He reached across and gave her long, yellow braid a little yank.

The next morning Slim and Jeannie leaned against the wood railings of the new corral fence attached to her barn. "All the mares are watered and fed. Do you want to turn them out?" Slim asked. "Diamond is poking his head over the pasture fence. He sure doesn't know what to think about those mares." Slim chuckled. "They'll all be his girlfriends soon."

"He'll be real bossy around them, too. He'll probably keep them close to his side," Jeannie said with a smile and a nod. "Yes, open the gate and let the mares out into the pasture."

Motioning to Vernon inside the corral to open the gate to the pasture, Slim entered the corral, lifted his hat, slapped it against his legs, and shooed the horses toward the open gate.

The mares trotted into the pasture toward Diamond. He greeted them by touching their noses and putting his neck across their necks in a show of friendly ownership. Then he nickered to them and raced away. The mares followed as Diamond led them deeper into the pasture toward the distant, wooded hills.

Slim joined Vernon in the barn for the morning chores. When Jeannie turned to go back to the ranch house, she noticed a rider loping his horse up the trail to the house. Turning around at the porch to get a better look, she saw it was Billy Joe's brother, Jack, bringing his horse to a stop at the hitching rail.

"Well, howdy, Jack," Jeannie said, shading her eyes against the morning sunlight. "How are you?"

"Oh, I'm fine," Jack said, dismounting and tying the reins of his horse to the front porch rail. He removed his hat. "How are you, Jeannie?"

"I'm doing good," Jeannie said, moving to the porch swing. "Come on and sit awhile." She motioned to the cane-bottomed chair on the porch.

"I rode over to see if you had time to show me around your ranch. I've been hearing a lot of good things about the goings-on around here," Jack said, smiling as he sat in the chair.

"Why, sure, I'll be glad to show you around," Jeannie said, returning his friendly smile. "We've been mighty busy around here, that's for sure."

"I'd enjoy hearing about it."

"All right, but how about a glass of buttermilk first?" Jeannie said, rising and going to the screen door. "Come on in, and I'll show you around the house, and then I'll have Slim saddle up his horse, Miss Sunrise, for me to ride. I've turned out a bunch of mares in the pasture with Diamond, and they've already run off to the hills somewhere."

When Jeannie told Slim she was going to give Jack a tour of the ranch, he watched as the couple rode away together, in the direction of the oaks and cedars, toward the hills, and the source of her water supply. For a moment, Jeannie turned and waved happily to her ranch foreman. Slim waved back, but he didn't smile. He watched until their horses faded into tiny specks. Then with a heavy-hearted sigh, he returned to his ranch chores.

Chapter 5
"A Fourth of July Picnic and A Surprise"

When Slim drew Jeannie's new buckboard to a halt at the Markham's hitching rail near the barn, Vernon hopped off the back and helped her down. Then Slim gave Jeannie her picnic basket of food.

"Thanks, boys," Jeannie said, as her ranch hands watched a group of men playing horseshoes beyond the barn. "I'm going to find Helga. I can see y'all are anxious to get into a game. Go and have fun."

"I shore plan on it," Vernon said, staring ahead at the game in progress. "Watch Billy Joe pitch that horseshoe. Whoa! He just made a ringer!" Vernon exclaimed. Several men patted a grinning Billy Joe on his back.

Jeannie shook her head and smiled. Billy Joe was at it again, showing off, as usual. She parted with the men and walked toward the house. Vernon and Slim strolled ahead to the gaming area, laughing and shoving one another in lighthearted friendship.

At the refreshment table shaded by a large oak tree, she waited while Mrs. Markham and Ma finished serving lemonade to several thirsty folks, who took their drinks and joined another couple sitting in cane-bottomed chairs under the shade of a smaller oak tree a short distance away.

"Congratulations on your fourth wedding anniversary, Mrs. Markham," Jeannie said.

"Why, thank you, Jeannie," Mrs. Markham said, beaming. "It's been a happy four years since you and Helga were pretty bridesmaids for me. And your sweet mutter was my beautiful maid of honor." She gave Ma a little pat on her shoulders.

"Howdy, Ma," Jeannie said, hugging her mother. "I'm glad to see you again."

Ma squeezed Jeannie back. "Hello, dear. Would you like some lemonade?" She gave Jeannie a glass.

"Thanks, Ma. It's such a warm day. I'm thirsty. Where's Helga?"

"She sees you," Mrs. Markham said, nodding toward the ranch house. "She's coming now."

Jeannie turned and watched her friend hurrying toward her. She's as pretty as ever, Jeannie thought. Helga's crème-colored hair hung loosely down her back. It was tied away from her face with a blue ribbon that matched her eyes and her light-blue organdy dress.

"Happy seventeenth birthday, Helga!" Jeannie cried, taking her friend's hands and holding her out at arms' length. "You look so pretty today!"

"Thank you, Jeannie. You always say such nice things to me," Helga said. "I'm glad to see you again. I don't like it that we don't have much time together anymore." Mrs. Markham gave Helga a glass of lemonade.

"Come, let's go sit in our favorite place—in the porch swing," Helga said with a lighthearted smile, leading the way back. "We have a lot to talk about."

"I know," Jeannie said. "I miss you. You must come and visit me soon."

"I will do that," Helga said, "now that I have passed my test and received my license to teach school." She sat down in the swing.

"Oh my grannies!" Jeannie screeched with delight, sitting beside Helga. She hugged her friend close, as if they were young children again. "You did it, Helga!"

Helga nodded happily. "I finally finished all my studies in Abilene, and I have been hired to replace Pastor Thompson at the country school. So, I will be close by."

"Helga, I'm so happy for you," Jeannie said. "Now we can visit each other again and sit on the porch and crochet and embroider and—"

"That is, if you can get away from your horses," Helga interrupted with a chuckle.

Jeannie rested her head on the back of the porch swing and said, "I'll admit the ranch keeps me busy, but I'll never be so busy that I can't visit with you, Helga." She patted her friend's arm affectionately. Together, in comfortable silence, they swung slowly in the porch swing, as they had often done, many times before, in their growing-up years.

When the warm sun was almost overhead, Pastor Thompson, acting as auctioneer, stood before food baskets covered with colorful luncheon tablecloths. "Now gather around, all you unmarried young men, and let us hear your bid on these wonderful baskets of delicious food prepared by the young ladies of the congregation. And let's all be generous in the bidding," Pastor said. "Remember, all the money will go to the Missionary Fund to help our missionaries in Africa and other foreign countries to bring the Gospel of Jesus Christ to the world."

There was good-natured jostling among the young men, struggling to remember the special basket prepared by the young lady of their choice. Pastor lifted a blue basket decorated with yellow flowers. "I know that basket," Billy Joe called. "I bid one dollar!"

"I have one dollar bid for this pretty basket. Do I hear another bid?" Pastor Thompson asked.

"I bid one dollar and fifty cents," Vernon shouted. He poked Slim in a mischievous way and whispered something in his ear.

Slim grinned and nodded.

"Two dollars!" Billy Joe shouted with a frown and a scowl at Vernon.

Vernon held up his hands and shrugged his shoulders.

"Do I hear two dollars and fifty cents?" Pastor Thompson asked.

Vernon shook his head "It's Billy Joe's basket," he said, smiling. "Just teasing him a little."

"Going—going—gone!" Pastor Thompson said. He lifted a tiny slip of paper hanging from the basket handle that identified the owner and read it. "Well, folks, Miss Helga Lengenfeld's basket sold to Billy Joe Jensen," he said. "Miss Lengenfeld, come forward, and join Mr. Jensen for his picnic-basket dinner."

A red-faced Helga stepped out from the crowd of young ladies and quickly joined Billy Joe. He carried her basket of food and offered her his free arm as they hurried to the shade of a distant oak tree.

Other picnic baskets were auctioned off, and each self-conscious young lady stepped forward to join the young man who had won her basket. Then the shy and embarrassed couple strolled to a shady area to enjoy the young lady's basket of food.

"Well, what have we here?" Pastor Thompson asked, lifting a white basket with miniature black cardboard horses decorating the sides. "Some young lady must certainly like horses," Pastor Thompson said with a twinkle in his eyes. "Now, who could she be?"

There were chuckles and murmurs all around, and several folks sent secretive glances in Jeannie's direction. Jeannie felt uncomfortable. She wished she could just go sit under a shade tree somewhere and eat with Ma and Pa. But that wouldn't be the thing to do. She wanted to support the missionary effort, so she'd have to eat with the young man who would win her basket.

"I bid two dollars."

It was Jack's voice. Jeannie looked at the crowd of young men and soon found him standing beside Slim. Then she heard Slim say, "Two fifty."

"Three dollars," Jack added quickly.

"Are there any other young men wishing to join in this bidding?" Pastor Thompson asked.

"Three seventy-five," Vernon said, smiling mischievously.

"Four dollars," Jack said, with a determined look on his face.

Jeannie found it hard to believe that anyone would give that much money for her basket of fried chicken. Grannies! Her cooking wasn't worth that much!

"Five dollars," Slim said, looking Jack in the eye.

Jack took a deep breath. "Ten dollars!" he said loudly.

Nervously, Jeannie twisted a strand of loose hair that had escaped from her long yellow braid. She twisted the strand around her forefinger. It was a childhood habit she occasionally returned to, when she was feeling anxious.

More than anything, Jeannie hoped Slim wouldn't risk any more money. She paid him fifteen dollars a month which was good wages for a ranch foreman, but she hoped he would stop bidding. It was foolishness for him to waste almost a month's wages on her food basket.

"Ten dollars!" Pastor Thompson almost shouted with delight. "Do I hear ten fifty?"

Slim sighed and pushed his hat back. Then he shrugged and reached over and shook Jack's hand. Jeannie watched him walk away to join Waco and Mr. Markham's other ranch hands at a picnic table Mrs. Markham had prepared for them. It seemed to her that Slim's face had a look of regret, but she couldn't be sure.

"Going—going—gone!" Pastor Thompson said, beaming. "Sold to Jack Jenkins. Come forward, Miss Jeannie Hanson, and join Mr. Jenkins for dinner," Pastor said, reading her name from the slip of paper attached to her basket. "And thank you, Mr. Jenkins, for your generous contribution to the Missionary Fund."

Jeannie knew her face was as red as any of the other girls' faces had been. She hurried to Jack and took his arm. He grinned from ear to ear, and led her to the distant shade tree where Helga and Billy Joe sat waiting.

"Did y'all have this planned all along?" Jeannie asked, watching a nervous Helga quickly spread her checkered tablecloth on the sun-dried prairie grass underneath the shady oak and begin digging in her picnic basket. She didn't look at Jeannie.

"Well, Jack told me he was going to win your basket, whatever it cost him," Billy Joe said, while Jeannie knelt and lifted her tablecloth cover from the basket.

Jack gave Jeannie a light-hearted wink and said, "Reckon I won the special pleasure of your company for dinner, Miss Jeannie." He sat down on the edge of the cloth that she had spread out and crossed his legs. "However, Slim gave me a run for my money," Jack admitted, removing his hat. "He had me scared for awhile."

Jeannie remembered the look on Slim's face as he walked away with his head downcast. For a moment she felt a little sorry for him. But right now, there was Jack to think about. He was holding out his plate, waiting patiently for her to fill it with fried chicken and potato salad.

When the sky darkened a little after dusk, Mr. Markham stood before the happy crowd of visiting folks. "Ladies and gentlemen," he said, "I'd like for everyone to please settle down."

He waited a few moments until the chatting and murmuring stopped. "Mrs. Markham and I have a proud announcement to make," he said, gazing at all the expectant faces. "Mr. Billy Joe Jenkins has requested the hand in marriage of our beautiful, little daughter, Helga. Her mother and I have consented to this union and, of course, so has our Helga."

Mr. Markham smiled, looked out over the crowd, and beckoned with one hand. "Billy Joe, Helga dear," he said, "please come and stand beside us and let our guests get a good look at you two young folks." Then, during the loud applause from the visitors gathered around, he shook hands with a beaming Billy Joe and hugged a blushing Helga standing beside her mother.

Mr. Markham turned and again addressed the crowd. "Y'all know this is Mrs. Markham's and my fourth wedding anniversary, and today, our Helga is seventeen on this wonderful Fourth of July holiday. We're happy y'all came to help us celebrate. We have a lot to be thankful for, and our hearts are full tonight," he said. "Now, folks, let's congratulate this beautiful and happy couple in a big way with three hip, hip hoorays!"

When the cheers died down, Mr. Markham shouted, "It's time for the fireworks to begin! Waco and Eagle Feather have prepared a fine display to help us celebrate the fact that we live in the United States of America. We're all mighty proud to live in the Lone Star State, in our beautiful West Texas. It's here, we have the best farming and grazing land in the whole USA, right folks?"

A great cheer rang out again, and all eyes looked upward as a burst of reds, blues and whites shot into the air, filling the night sky overhead.

Jeannie stood beside Jack in shocked delight, mulling over Mr. Markham's surprise announcement. She watched her dearest friend holding hands with Billy Joe and crossed to her, and gently touched her shoulders. "Congratulations, Helga," she murmured, giving her a hug. "But why did you keep your secret from me?" Jeannie's voice, although friendly, held a touch of hurt. "Why didn't you tell me?" she asked. Her eyes were filled with confusion.

"Well, Poppa and Billy Joe wanted me to keep it a secret until Poppa could make the announcement tonight," Helga explained, hugging her friend close. She bit her lower lip as she had always done when she was nervous. "Oh, Jeannie," she said softly, lowering her eyes, "I wanted to tell you all day! I'm so sorry."

"It's all right," Jeannie said, hugging back. "I understand. I knew you had something on your mind, but I had no idea it was your engagement."

"Well, what I'm going to say now is no secret," Helga said firmly, looking her friend in the eyes. "You will be my maid of honor at my December wedding, and no excuses about it!"

"Grannies! If you think for one minute I wouldn't be your maid of honor, you have another thought a'coming!" Jeannie exclaimed.

She turned to Billy Joe. Suddenly, she felt mischievous. She shook her head and groaned. With a heavy sigh and a pretense of concern, she looked at him and said, "Oh, Helga, I don't know how you're EVER going to put up with Billy Joe and his tricky ways. I'm sure he's going to be a trial for you, just like he was during our school days!"

Then Jeannie smiled and gave a grinning Billy Joe a big hug. "Congratulations, old friend," she said. "You finally won her." A thoughtful look crossed her face. "You know," she said with a twinkle in her eyes, "I think it must have been all those duets you two sang together at parties and celebrations through the years that helped you win her." Jeannie paused a moment, and in a more serious voice said, "Actually, you both sing great harmony together. I'm sure your life together will be the same."

"Much obliged," Billy Joe said softly.

Jeannie studied him closely. Why, it seemed that he was about to cry! She could see the glint of tears. She knew Billy Joe had been smitten with Helga ever since he first laid eyes on her, way back there, that first day when Helga entered school with them. No doubt, for him—today was the best day in his life. "All teasing aside, Billy Joe, I know y'all will be mighty happy together," Jeannie said.

Turning to Helga, she patted her friend's arm and said, "Isn't it wonderful that we've all been friends for so many years?"

"Ja, (yes)," Helga said, returning to her German language, "I do love all my good friends."

"And we all love you," Jeannie said, smiling warmly. Then she and her childhood friends, together in fond companionship, watched the colorful Fourth of July fireworks continue to light up the starry, night sky.

Chapter 6
"Jeannie's Birthday Party"

Jeannie carefully slipped her doeskin dress over her two yellow braids and stared at herself in the mirror. It was true, if it weren't for her freckles and blonde hair, and of course, her blue eyes, she'd look like a Comanche Indian maiden, for sure. She thought about her birthday a few years ago when Prairie Flower's mother, Little Fawn, had given her the dress.

Gently touching the beaded decorations, Jeannie remembered the excitement on Prairie Flower's face when she proudly said she had sewn them on the birthday dress herself. With a happy sigh, Jeannie gave her hair a final pat and murmured, "Today, November 10, 1889, you are eighteen years old, young lady. Now, you are all grown up."

But she felt a twinge of uncertainty when she turned away from the mirror and slipped on the moccasins Gray Wolf had helped tan and soften. Smiling, Jeannie recalled Little Fawn's words. "Your feet like mine. They are big."

Jeannie wiggled her toes and stared down at her feet. Little Fawn had been right about her feet. They sure weren't small and dainty. Working all day long on a ranch, tramping around outside in her cowboy boots, wasn't lady-like and didn't help her feet any, but that was ranch life. There wasn't much she could do about it.

Slim sat waiting on Miss Sunrise when Jeannie stepped out on the front porch. He gave her Diamond's reins. "I know you don't need any help mounting up, Miss Indian Princess," Slim said. "I reckon, you must know how much I enjoy seeing you wear that pretty fringed dress."

"Yes, I do know. Thank you, Slim," Jeannie said, mounting Diamond. "I like wearing it. And I like riding on this comfortable saddle you gave me on my birthday. I remember it was the same day Little Fawn gave me this dress."

"Ma'am, it's happiness itself to see you riding on that saddle," Slim said as they turned their mounts and headed down the trail. "I'm glad it gives you enjoyment."

Jeannie breathed in deeply and watched several black hawks soaring lazily about in the sky. "It's mighty nice of Mr. Markham to give me a birthday party today," she said.

"Well, now, Miss Helga's your best friend, and it's my opinion, Mr. Markham likes to get folks together for a party whenever he can," Slim said, reaching in his pocket for a cedar twig. He let it dangle in his mouth like a toothpick.

"Maybe so," Jeannie said. "I've seen him laughing and having a big time, enjoying himself visiting and talking with all the neighbors at his parties." She looked up at the blue sky. "I'm glad we're riding over there on our horses. It's a real pretty afternoon."

"It is, for a fact," Slim said.

Jeannie watched a hawk swoop down in the nearby pasture. The others quickly followed. Jeannie decided they probably had found a little critter or some kind of rodent.

Nearing the Markham ranch, Slim rubbed his chin for a moment and looked across to Jeannie. "I'm sure hoping you'll save me a dance this evening, Little Lady," he said.

Jeannie shook her head, sighed, and fixed her gaze on him. "After all these years, Slim, I reckon, you should know how I feel about dancing, by now." She grinned good-naturedly and shrugged. "But, if you don't mind me stepping all over your feet, and you don't twirl me around too fast and get me all pie-eyed and dizzy, I reckon, we can dance one," she said.

Slim politely touched his forefinger to his hat brim. "I'm much obliged, ma'am," he said. "I'll look forward to it."

Helga waited on the front porch until Jeannie dismounted. Then she gave her a hug and led her to the swing while Slim took the horses to the hitching rail at the barn.

"Happy eighteenth birthday, 'Miss Horse Ranch Lady,'" Helga said. "How are things at the ranch? I haven't seen you in a month or so, but it seems like a year."

"I know," Jeannie said joining Helga in the swing. "I miss you, too. Teaching school keeps you busy."

"And grading compositions and schoolwork at night," Helga added.

Jeannie raised her eyebrows in a knowing way. "Uh-huh," she said. "And also courting with Billy Joe in your free time. I reckon, you've forgotten all about me, your very best friend."

Helga bit her lower lip. "Now, dot's not true, Jeannie," she said nervously, reverting back to her German accent. "I haven't forgotten about you. So don't say dot. We should be talking about my wedding next month. Mutter is sewing my dress for me."

Jeannie saw she had upset Helga. Feeling regretful, she patted Helga's hand and said, "Ma told me about your dress when I went to visit her last week, and I want you to know, she's already started sewing my dress, too."

"Goot!" Helga said happily. "I am getting so excited about my wedding, but you haven't answered my question."

"What question?"

"You know—the one about your ranch, Jeannie. What have you been doing all this time?"

"Oh, nothing much," Jeannie said, lazily resting her head back against the porch swing. "I sleep until ten o'clock in the morning. Then my maid brings me a tray with buttermilk and eggs, so I can take my time eating my breakfast in bed." Her eyes were twinkling merrily. "Then she helps me dress and comb my hair—"

"Jeannie, be serious," Helga interrupted. "I want the truth."

Jeannie sighed. "The truth is– my sweet little friend from Germany—the truth is, I get up before sunrise. I cook breakfast for Slim and Vernon and sometimes his little brother Eli. While they are eating, the boys and Slim talk about the day's work, and I tidy up the kitchen. Do you want me to go on?"

"Ja, sure," Helga said. "I want to know."

"Then, I feed the chickens and do any other chores around the place that need doing."

"How are the horses?"

"They are fine," Jeannie said, sitting up, "really fine. And guess what?"

"What?"

"I'm expecting some new baby colts in the spring. Diamond has been busy being a husband to my mares. In fact, Slim told me Miss Sunrise will drop a colt, too!"

"Well, my goodness, isn't that nice," Helga said with a happy smile. "I think that makes you and Slim like a family—"

"Now, Helga," Jeannie said with a touch of warning in her voice, "don't start trying to be a match-maker."

"Who me? Never." Helga said innocently. "Come, let's go to the party." She took Jeannie's arm. "Billy Joe is playing his banjo, and folks will be dancing soon. See, Mutter and your ma are busy serving food already."

"They love to feed the folks," Jeannie said, nearing the refreshment table.

"Happy birthday, Jeannie," Mrs. Markham said, coming around the table to give Jeannie a hug.

"Thank you, Mrs. Markham," Jeannie said, hugging back.

"Give me a kiss," Ma said, reaching out to Jeannie. "You look mighty pretty this evening."

"Thanks, Ma," Jeannie said. She gave her mother a warm hug and then kissed her on her cheek. "Where's Pa?"

"He and Henry are sitting with the menfolks, over there under that oak tree. I imagine they're talking farm-talk."

"Jeannie! Jeannie! Happy birthday!"

Jeannie turned to see Prairie Flower running toward her. She leaned down and gave the young girl a hug. "Thank you, Prairie Flower. My grannies! You are getting tall! You almost touch my shoulders now."

Prairie Flower smiled and nodded. "When I'm finished with my schooling, I will come and help you on the ranch, like I promised you a long time ago."

"I will need your help by then, I'm sure," Jeannie said. "You can come and help me in the summer months if you want to."

"I want to," Prairie Flower said. "Mother is watching the little children. Come and play 'Go in and Out the Windows' with the rest of us." She pulled at Jeannie's hand.

"Let's go, Helga," Jeannie said, chuckling. "The young'uns have seen us now. Melissa, Esther, and the twins, Pearl and Ruby, are beckoning to us."

"Gray Wolf wants to be the farmer," Prairie Flower revealed, "so he can choose Melissa to be his wife."

Jeannie remembered when she had first taught the children to play the game. A younger Gray Wolf had been the farmer then and had chosen Melissa as his wife. It seemed he still was sweet on the little girl.

"The children are growing up fast, aren't they, Helga?" Jeannie said as she and Helga joined in a circle with them.

"Ja, I see it happening every day at school," Helga said. "I have to keep my eyes on Gray Wolf. He is always trying to do something mischievous to get Melissa's attention."

"Just like someone else I knew in school, and now you are marrying him," Jeannie said with a smile. "Billy Joe used to upset you so much."

With an impatient toss of her head, Helga rolled her eyes upward. "He certainly did do that," she agreed. "And sometimes, he still does!" she added with a playful smile.

Later, at the refreshment table, Jeannie sipped her cup of punch and gazed ahead to the wooden dance platform and beyond to the risers where Billy Joe, holding his banjo, sat beside the fiddlers and other musicians. With his accordion strapped to his shoulders, Vernon and Eli Wilson's father sat beside Billy Joe, and Helga sat on Billy Joe's other side. Helga had already sung harmony with Billy Joe on several tunes they always enjoyed performing together.

When the musicians struck up the beginning chords of a waltz, Jeannie glimpsed Jack approaching. He tipped his hat and extended his hand. "Evening, Jeannie," he said. "I believe this is our dance."

Jeannie smiled politely and gave her cup to Ma and followed Jack up the platform steps.

"Happy eighteenth," Jack said, as they glided out on the floor.

"Thank you, Jack," Jeannie said, concentrating on following his lead. "How's the farm doing?"

"Keeps me busy," Jack said. "Pa's thinking of planting more cotton in the spring. How's the horse ranch?"

"I'm expecting most of my mares to drop foals in the spring."

Jack nodded. "Congratulations! That's good news." He was silent for a moment. Then he looked down at her and asked, "Would you ever consider farming some of your land or maybe raising cattle on it?"

"Nope!" Jeannie said, almost too emphatically. She gazed back at Jack and explained, "Land's not good soil for farming. Maybe, longhorns, later on."

"I see," Jack said in a dejected voice. He sighed. "I sure wish you liked farming."

Recognizing his disappointment, Jeannie said, "I'm sorry, Jack. I just love horses. You should know that by now."

"I reckon so," Jack murmured as they circled around. "Miss Jeannie," he said with a twinkle in his eyes, "did I tell you how pretty you look this evening?"

Jeannie felt her cheeks turning red. She lowered her eyes.

"Remember that night when you first wore your deerskin dress? It caused quite a fuss with some of the folks, especially the Deckers who'd lost a young son years ago to the Comanches."

"I remember," Jeannie said. "There's Mrs. Decker over there." Jeannie smiled and nodded to the elderly, gray-haired woman as they danced past. Mrs. Decker smiled and lifted a white crocheted, gloved-covered hand and gave a little wave to Jeannie.

"Mr. Markham and Pa helped them change their way of thinking about Indians," Jeannie said. The music ended, and they stepped down to the outside area. "Mr. Markham praised Eagle Feather and his family as an example of peaceful Comanches and talked about how we're all trying to get along now."

"It's working out fine, too," Jack said. "There were losses and sorrows on both sides during the settlement of the Texas plains. I'm glad it's all over now." He leaned his back against the side railing that circled the dance platform and faced Jeannie.

"I'm glad it's over, too," Jeannie said, running her finger along a small part of the smooth, wood railing. "I know when I was younger I felt afraid, and I didn't like the thought of Comanches, especially when some bad ones stole Diamond. We got him back, though," she said, gazing at Jack.

"I heard about that," he said, pushing up his hat brim and resting a booted foot against the platform sideboards.

"The next year when Eagle Feather told me it was a few bad Indian braves who had disobeyed their chief and gone out on a raiding party, then I understood," Jeannie said. "And I changed my way of thinking." On the stage beyond, she saw Helga rise and stand beside Billy Joe. "Let's listen," Jeannie said. "They're going to sing now."

Jack turned and looked at the stage. "My brother shore is love struck," he said, grinning and leaning his arms on the railing. "Helga has always been special to him."

Jeannie nodded, "Like a bear following a honey bee to a honey tree."

Jack chuckled. "That's good," he said. "And true, for a fact!" He looked across to Jeannie. "Course, I'm standing beside a might nice young lady, who is special to me," he said softly.

Jeannie felt her face flaming red again. "Thank you, Jack. Come on," she said, hoping to draw Jack's attention away from herself. "Let's listen to those two songbirds sing together."

As the evening drew to a close, Jeannie expressed her thanks to Mr. and Mrs. Markham and to their guests for attending her birthday party. Waiting patiently until Jeannie had given good-bye hugs to her parents and Henry and Linda Mae, Helga pulled her aside and said softly, "I watched you dancing with Jack, and later on, I watched Slim and you dancing. I saw the way they both looked at you, Jeannie. I'm very sure they are thinking serious thoughts about you."

"Grannies, Helga!" Jeannie exclaimed under her breath. "There you go again." Yet, for the first time, she felt a bit uncomfortable. Maybe there was some truth in what her best friend was saying. "Well, I certainly hope they are not thinking 'serious thoughts' about me," she said firmly. "I don't have time to be 'a-sparking and spooning' my time away. I'm too busy."

"I know you are busy," Helga continued in a confidential tone, "but I think you should be ready. One of these days you might get a proposal of marriage from either Jack or Slim, or maybe from both of them."

Jeannie looked ahead to see Slim approaching on Miss Sunrise, and leading Diamond by his reins. Slim offered her the reins.

"Good night, Helga," Jeannie said, with an amused chuckle. She gave her friend a fond, little peck on her cheek.

"You worry too much about me." She patted Helga's shoulder. "I'll be looking for you to come over soon, so we can talk and plan some more for your wedding coming up next month." She turned and mounted Diamond.

"Ja, we do that, Jeannie. I'll be visiting you soon," Helga said, waving goodbye. Jeannie waved back, and she and Slim turned their mounts down the trail to the ranch gate that opened out on the wagon road home.

Chapter 7
"Spring Babies"

"Where has the time gone, Helga?" Jeannie asked her visiting friend as they sat together in Jeannie's porch swing. Junior lay stretched out near the wide, wooden porch steps dozing.

"I don't know. It seems like just yesterday you were my dear maid of honor and Prairie Flower was my sweet little bridesmaid in my December wedding. And now it's already the middle of April," Helga said.

It was a mighty pretty wedding," Jeannie said, with a thoughtful look in her eyes as she gazed about her green pastureland, pausing, on several of her beautiful mares and colts grazing under shady oak trees in the distance. Happily, she turned back to her friend and said, "You were such a beautiful bride."

"Thank you, Jeannie, and weren't the twins, Ruby and Pearl, adorable flower girls? They dropped all those little rose petals on the church aisle as they walked ahead of me. You know they made them at school. They used red crayons and cut and colored rose petals all afternoon," Helga said. "Since it was winter time, we had no fresh flowers."

Jeannie smiled and said, "Everyone appreciated their special idea for your wedding. They are clever little girls. And I almost laughed out loud when I saw the serious way your little three-year-old brother, Frankie, walked down the aisle, very slowly and carefully, holding the little, white satin pillow with the wedding rings on it. He is so cute. He looks just like his pa."

"He keeps Mutter very busy now," Helga said. "He loves to run outside and play with Gray Wolf, but Gray Wolf is growing up fast. He doesn't have much time to play with a little boy."

"He's over there in the corral now, helping Slim and the boys brand the young colts," Jeannie said. "He's anxious to become one of my cowboys, so I allow him to work part-time, but he knows he must finish his schooling."

"I think so, too," Helga said. "I saw Slim and Vernon and Eli working when I rode up on Morning Star."

"Pa and my brother Henry are also working, and your pa sent over Waco and Eagle Feather to help out. I'm much obliged for their help, too." Jeannie said. "You be sure and tell your pa, I said that."

"Oh, Poppa was glad to send you some help today." Then Helga sighed. "Eventually, I hope Billy Joe and I get a place of our own. For now, we have to live with Poppa and Mutter because it's close to school for me; and Billy Joe can ride his horse to town to work at Mr. Davidson's bank."

"Would you ever want to teach school in town?" Jeannie asked.

"No," Helga said, shaking her head. "I want to stay in the country. The children need me here. Besides, I don't think I'm a town person. I like the country."

"It grows on you. That's a fact," Jeannie agreed. "As for me, I never want to live in town. I need my 'elbow room.' And now that I have my own ranch, I want to take care of my animals."

Prairie Flower stepped out on the porch carrying a bucket and a dipper. "I made lemonade for the menfolks," she said.

"Well, thank you, Prairie Flower," Jeannie said. "Sit down and rest. Did you find everything you needed in the kitchen?"

"Yes ma'am, I did," Prairie Flower said, sitting in a cane-bottomed chair near the swing. Junior rose and flopped down beside her. He pushed his nose into her hand. "I love to work in your kitchen. I will be happy when I finish school. Then I can work for you all the time."

"I'll be mighty proud to have you, Prairie Flower. But you just keep up with your studies. You'll be glad someday that you did, won't she, Helga?"

"Yes, indeed, you will, Prairie Flower. You are a good student."

"Thank you, Mrs. Jenkins," Prairie Flower said, patting Junior's head.

"By the way, Helga," Jeannie said, turning her gaze to her friend. "I love the Edgar Allen Poe books you gave me when you returned from your honeymoon trip to Dallas. I think I own his entire collection now—thanks to you." Jeannie patted Helga's arm affectionately. "I'm also glad you gave me Mark Twain's latest book. I'm enjoying reading *A Connecticut Yankee in King Arthur's Court*. Thank you again, and thanks for my journal, too."

"I'm very happy you like the books," Helga said, smiling. "I know you are a 'book worm.'"

Jeannie chuckled. "Yes, I am for sure." Then she yawned and rose. "Well, girls, maybe we should stop being lazy and take the menfolks some cool lemonade."

"Mutter sent over these doughnuts," Helga said, reaching down for her hand-woven basket covered with an embroidered tea towel.

"They'll like that," Jeannie said. "May I put a couple of them in the kitchen for us?"

"Of course, take the basket, and after we finish with the menfolks, we'll come back and enjoy our lemonade and doughnuts on the porch."

Helga gave the basket to Jeannie, and the girls entered the house followed by Junior. He sniffed and wagged his tail and stared at the basket in Jeannie's hand.

"Be sure and take a doughnut out for Junior," Helga said. "A little bit of sweets won't hurt him. He's a good dog, aren't you, boy?" Helga patted his head, and Junior wagged his tail happily.

"As long as you can keep your eyes on him, he's a pretty good dog," Jeannie said, chuckling. "He sure loves to chase little critters though, especially skunks."

Jeannie glanced at the basket again. "I see you covered the basket top with one of the tea towels I embroidered for your wedding shower."

"Ja, it has cute little puppies on it. They are the children of Ole Blue and Lady," Helga said. When Jeannie put the basket on the kitchen cabinet counter, Helga lifted the towel and opened it to its full length. "You even embroidered their names underneath the puppies," she said pointing to their names. "Old Blue Jr., Princess, and Cutie Pie."

Jeannie lifted a few doughnuts from the basket and set them on a plate. "Ole Blue had another son; Billy Joe's, Hunter, but I got a little tired of sewing puppy names," she admitted.

"Ja," Helga said, "Ole Blue and Lady had a big family. Even though Hunter is missing from the design, it's still a very pretty tea towel."

That night before she blew out her kerosene lamp, Jeannie settled into bed with her journal and pencil. She propped up her knees and began to write:

Had a wonderful visit with Helga. Prairie Flower made lemonade and tidied up the kitchen. Slim said Gray

Wolf was a good hand with the colts. He rides and ropes well. Mr. Markham sent over Waco and Eagle Feather to help out. Pa and Henry were here, too. Ma stayed home because she was doing a'washing. Mrs. Markham sent doughnuts for the men.

I am so thankful for all those good folks who gave me a hand today. I love my horses and my ranch. Diamond, my faithful stallion, has sired some beautiful baby colts. I adore them and treasure them all. I am truly blessed!

Thank you God.

P.S. Pa has a bad cold and a cough. I told him I didn't think he should have come today, but he said he wanted to help out. Before he went home I told him to let Ma doctor him up with some hot tea and lemon, and then he should gargle with warm salt water. I hope he does, but I know Pa. He thinks he doesn't need doctoring like the rest of us folks. He just nodded and winked at me. Then he yanked on my long braid like he always does whenever he gets the chance!

Jeannie closed her journal and blew out the lamp. She was tired but happy. It had been a wonderful day!

Chapter 8
"Pa's Illness"

When a loud clap of thunder sounded in the middle of the night, Jeannie awoke with a start. She sprang out of bed and stood at the window. Long, jagged flashes of lightning shot across the sky and sheets of heavy rain pelted on the roof of her ranch house. Little rivulets of water drops slithered down her windowpane. She turned back to bed and pulled the covers up around her neck. It was a good thing the ranch hands had finished branding the little colts yesterday. It looked like this part of West Texas was in for a good rain.

The following day when Slim and Vernon hurried into breakfast after their chores in the barn, Slim said, "It's probably going to rain for a few days. The sky is mighty dark, and there's no sign of a let up."

"I reckon so," Jeannie said. "It's a late storm, but it seems like a good one. You boys might as well go back to the bunkhouse and relax. I'm sure there's no work y'all can get done today."

"Sounds good to me," Slim said. "Vernon, how about a game of cards? When we get tired of that we can play checkers or dominoes."

It rained for several days before a bright morning sun peeked over the oak trees in the east. After Jeannie finished her chores, Slim saddled Diamond and brought him to her. "I'll try and be back by supper time," Jeannie said, taking the reins and mounting. "But if I'm not, there's ham and beans in the cooler for you and Vernon."

"We'll make out fine," Slim said. "You have a nice visit."

Jeannie sighed and said, "I'm worried about Pa's cold, so I'm going over to see how he's doing. If it gets too late, I might spend the night with my folks."

"Stay as long as you want to. Vernon and I will check on the horses today."

"Thanks," Jeannie said. "I know I can depend on your help, Slim."

Slim nodded. "You betcha," he said. "You can for a fact." He gave Diamond a little pat on his rump, and Jeannie turned him around on the trail to the road.

After Jeannie put Diamond in a stall in the barn, she hurried to the house. "Howdy, Ma," she said.

Ma held out her arms and hugged Jeannie. "Come in, dear," she said.

"How's Pa's cold?" Jeannie asked, entering the parlor.

"He's feeling poorly." There was worry in Ma's voice. "I told him not to go out in the rain that day it rained so hard, but he said he couldn't let all the chores go by." Listening, Jeannie followed Ma to the kitchen. "His cold got worse, and now, he has a bad cough and congestion in his chest."

Jeannie sighed. "Oh, grannies! What are you doing for him, Ma?" she asked with a look of concern.

"Well, I made him go to bed, and that wasn't easy." Ma shook her head. She lifted her hands in and out of her apron pockets nervously.

"Knowing Pa, I'm sure it wasn't," Jeannie agreed.

"I put a mustard plaster on his chest. He didn't want it, but I put it on him anyway. And I also rubbed his chest with ointment."

Jeannie shed her coat and entered the bedroom where Pa lay sleeping. She listened to his labored breathing for a moment and then tiptoed out of the room. "Ma, I think we need Little Fawn's help. She might know some kind of herbs that will ease his breathing. I'm going to ride over to the Markham ranch and bring her back here."

"All right, dear," Ma said with a heavy sigh. "I'm beginning to worry about Pa. And stop by Henry's place. Tell him we need him to come over and milk Lu-Lu."

When Little Fawn entered the bedroom, Pa was awake, but his face was pale. After touching his forehead, she looked at Ma and Jeannie and said, "Face hot. Needs to sweat. Must heat water and put on floor in pots. Put sheet over him and pots. Then steam get inside sheet and help him breathe. I make good medicine for him to drink now."

Throughout the day, Little Fawn, Ma, and Jeannie nursed Pa. His fever lessened and his body cooled, but his breathing did not improve. As evening drew near, it seemed to worsen. Little Fawn held a spoon of heated herb vapors close to Pa's nostrils. "Breathe in," she said. "Will help lungs."

Silent tears rolled down Ma's face. "I'm afraid he has pneumonia," she whispered to Jeannie.

Jeannie fought back tears. "Oh, Pa," she groaned softly, watching his labored breathing.

A short time later Ma, Jeannie, and Henry gathered outside the closed bedroom door.

"Pa's lungs are filling up with fluid," Ma said softly. "He can hardly breathe. Little Fawn and I have done all we can think of to do." Ma's voice broke as she went on, "But he's not doing well. Everything is in God's hands now."

Tears welled up in Ma's eyes. Henry put his arms around his mother and patted her back. "Try and get some rest, Ma. You're tired," he said. "Go lie down on the bed in my old room for a while. I'll call you if there's any change."

"All right, Son," Ma said. "I'll rest for just a few minutes."

Several days later, sitting beside Ma, and Henry and Linda Mae, in the sanctuary of Pastor Thompson's church, Jeannie listened to Helga's sweet soprano voice, singing a beautiful new hymn for Pa's funeral.

" 'There's a land that is fairer than day
And by faith we can see it afar
For the Father waits over the way
To prepare us a dwelling place there.

In the sweet by and by
We shall meet on that beautiful shore
In the sweet by and by
We shall meet on that beautiful shore.' "

"Oh, Pa," Jeannie whispered sadly. "Why did you go out to work in the heavy rain when you had such a bad cold?" She choked back a grieving sob, and glanced at Ma. She was wiping her tearful eyes with a handkerchief.

The church was filled with friends from all around the community. Jeannie's gaze took in the lovely wild flowers in fruit jars everywhere in the room. A bouquet of bluebonnets and yellow buttercups lay on Pa's casket.

When Helga finished singing, several men rose and shared their memories of Pa. They spoke about his many good qualities. Mr. Markham talked about Pa's loyal friendship through the years. He praised his good neighborly ways and his willingness to give a helping hand—at any time—day or night.

Then Pastor Thompson spoke and concluded his eulogy for Pa by saying, "I'm sure God has a special place for this good Christian man in heaven with Him. As in the words of that beautiful hymn, our dear Helga sang, 'In the sweet by and by—we shall meet on that beautiful shore,' be assured, beloved ones, we shall all meet again in God's heaven."

When all the folks went home later in the day—leaving behind bountiful dishes of every kind of tasty food for the grieving family—Ma, Jeannie, Henry and Linda Mae visited Pa's grave once more. Then Henry and Linda Mae slowly walked Ma back to the house for a much-needed rest.

But Jeannie lingered awhile and sat between the graves of Pa and Ole Blue. "Well, Pa," she whispered, "you and Ole Blue are side by side now. And I reckon your spirits are together up in heaven. So I know you'll be looking out for one another and doing what you can to be helpful and obedient to God's wishes."

Jeannie gently touched the colorful wild flowers, covering both mounds of earth. She patted Pa's grave. "Don't worry none, Pa. Henry and I will see that Ma is taken care of." Jeannie's voice broke. "It's just so hard to know you're not here anymore. I feel so alone," she murmured. Tears rolled down her cheeks. Then she gulped and sighed. "I know you want me to be brave and strong for you, Pa," she said. "So, I'll try."

Thoughts tumbled about in her memory as Jeannie recalled shared times with Pa. She remembered their trip together in the wagon for supplies at Wasserman's trading post that had now grown into the community of Shinoaks. On the way home, she hid under the wagon seat when Pa told her he saw Comanches coming on horseback, and they sometimes took little blonde girls and raised them. Fortunately, the Comanches only wanted sugar. Finding none, they turned their ponies and left. Jeannie was safe.

Then there was the time, one night, when bad Indians stole Pa's horses, including her Diamond. Pa was angry because Jeannie followed him secretly, but he allowed her to stay and help out when Mr. Markham and his ranch hands met them along the Leon River. The horses were recovered and Diamond was once again safe in the barn.

Then there was the day after the terrible cyclone that Pa and Mr. Markham hunted the mountain lion that attacked Diamond and her. The lion missed them, and they got away. Pa and Mr. Markham went after the mountain lion, and Pa shot and killed it.

Jeannie sighed and rose. She must go to the house and help out. She felt a little better. At least her head was full of so many different things she had shared with Pa, and she could always recall their special times together. That way, Pa would live forever in her very own precious memories.

Chapter 9
"Good News"

Jeannie sat in the porch swing with Junior at her side. Lost in thoughts of Pa, she alternately patted and ruffled Junior's smooth, gray coat. He lifted his head and licked her face. Then he lay his head in her lap. "Good dog, Junior," Jeannie said. "You know I'm feeling sad, today, don't you?"

Junior gazed up at her with his big brown eyes and made a little whimpering noise.

"You understand don't you," Jeannie said, holding Junior's face gently between her hands.

Junior thumped his tail slowly. Suddenly, he lifted his head and pricked up his ears. He sat on his haunches and stared down the trail. "Is someone coming?" Jeannie asked, searching the path between the oak trees leading to the road.

"My grannies! It's Morning Star and Helga," Jeannie cried, springing out of the swing to greet her best friend. She joined Junior on the porch steps. "Look, boy," Jeannie said. "Helga is bringing your sister, Cutie Pie, to play with you."

"Hello, Jeannie," Helga called. She drew Morning Star to a halt at the hitching rail.

"Get down, and sit with me," Jeannie said. "I'm mighty glad to see you."

Holding her small basket in one hand, Helga dismounted and said, "Now Cutie Pie, you and Junior can go run and play together." When she stepped on the porch, Junior dashed past and touched noses with Cutie Pie. Soon the two dogs were chasing one another in a game of tag.

"We're so glad your brother Henry offered to sell us his property," Helga said, following Jeannie to the swing. "We've been busy moving into the house. And now, you and I are real neighbors."

"I'm as tickled as a bullfrog in a dry creek tasting his first drop of rain," Jeannie said, smiling. "It pleases me greatly that you have Henry's home place."

"Billy Joe's very happy that Henry agreed to work the land for him," Helga said. "Now Billy Joe can continue working at the bank in Shinoaks."

"Well, Henry wanted y'all to have a place of your own. He's able to farm Pa's land and your place. And he's able to look after Ma, too," Jeannie said. "Y'all are family to us."

"Ja, and we love you folks, too," Helga said, patting Jeannie's arm. She sat beside her friend, taking pleasure in their comfortable companionship. For a moment, the two friends quietly enjoyed the warmth of the afternoon as they watched their pets playing a fast game of chase and tag.

Then Helga turned to Jeannie and asked, "How have you been doing these past few weeks, since you lost your precious pa?"

"To tell the truth, it's not been easy for me, Helga," Jeannie murmured.

Helga hugged her friend and patted her on her back. "I know, dear," she said softly. "Your pa was a good man, and you two were very close."

"We were," Jeannie said, brushing away a tear. "I'm glad he's buried next to Ole Blue. I know they are looking out for each other in heaven."

"I think so, too." Helga continued on, "You know my mutter gave me some fresh peaches the other day. I made a peach pie and some fried chicken for you and put them in my little basket. We can have a picnic lunch."

"Why, thank you, Helga," Jeannie said. "That's so thoughtful of you."

"How is your sweet mother doing these days?" Helga asked.

"She's not so lonely, now that Henry and Linda Mae and little Matthew have moved in with her." Jeannie chuckled. "Little Matthew is always underfoot. Ma loves that. And Princess has little Matthew's dog, Belle, for a playmate."

"I'm glad to hear your mother is doing better now," Helga said. She leaned close to her friend and whispered, "Jeannie, I have some wonderful news." There was a special glow on her face. "I can't wait to tell you."

"What news?"

"Oh, I'm so happy!" Helga squealed with delight. "Billy Joe and I are going to have a baby this coming December."

"Helga!" Jeannie exclaimed. "That IS wonderful news!" She hugged her best friend close.

"Ja," Helga said, her face flushed with excitement, "maybe it will be a Christmas baby."

"Maybe it will! I'm so pleased for you!" Jeannie cried. "Come in the house and let's have a piece of your delicious peach pie and a glass of buttermilk." Jeannie took Helga by the arm and led her into the house. "You know, I think I will get started right away and crochet a pretty little blanket for your new little one."

Chapter 10
"Helga's Sadness"

In the middle of a Saturday afternoon, several days later, Jeannie heard a loud knocking on her front porch door. She hurried to open it. Her brother Henry stood before her holding his hat in his hands.

"Why, Henry, come on in," Jeannie said, noticing Henry's white-faced look. "You don't have to knock."

Henry stepped inside. "I have some real bad news, Jeannie," he said, touching Jeannie's arm. "Helga's lost her baby—"

Jeannie put her hand over her mouth and gasped. "Oh no!" she exclaimed. "That's awful."

Henry nodded. "Helga's crying and carrying on something terrible," he said. "Her mother is with her at the house. Ma said for me to come and get you. And she wants Slim to ride into town and get Billy Joe."

"Slim's at the barn. Tell him to ride to town as fast as he can after he saddles up Miss Sunrise," Jeannie said, removing her apron. "And, Henry, please saddle Diamond for me while I get ready."

In the bedroom, Helga's mother and Ma stood aside for Jeannie. Giving them a quick nod, she hurried to sit at Helga's bedside. The face of her friend was grief-stricken and tear-stained, and her pale blonde hair was tangled and uncombed as she crumpled into Jeannie's outstretched arms.

"Jeannie, Jeannie," Helga moaned between sobs, "I lost my baby. I lost my baby."

Jeannie rocked her friend gently and held her close. "I'm so sorry, Helga. I'm so sorry," Jeannie whispered with tear-filled eyes. She glanced at Mrs. Markham and Ma standing in the doorway. They looked tired and exhausted. "I'll stay with her now," Jeannie said.

Mrs. Markham nodded wearily. "Come, Ruthie," she said. "I'll make hot tea for us." The two older women turned and left the room.

"Helga, dear, can you tell me what happened?" Jeannie asked softly.

Helga lay her head back on her pillow. "I'll try," she said, taking a deep breath. She gulped and wiped her nose on her handkerchief. "Well, it was such a nice day, so I decided to go to the bank to have lunch with Billy Joe," she began softly. "After lunch I was riding back on the trail. Morning Star was loping along, and we were almost home. Suddenly, he stepped in a prairie dog hole and stumbled. I went flying over his head and landed on my back." Helga shuddered.

"And Morning Star—I think his leg is broken," she said tearfully. "He can't get up. I tried to help him, but my stomach was hurting so much, I had to leave him lying back there on the wagon road a mile or so from here. I walked as fast as I could to your ma's place." Helga blew her nose and continued, "Your mother took one look at me. She sent Henry to get Mutter and Little Fawn, and then she drove me home in her buggy."

Helga lay back down and pulled the covers close. "I began having more pains. Mutter and Little Fawn arrived just in time. They helped me through it all." Helga closed her eyes for a moment and said, "Afterward, Little Fawn mixed up some herbs for me. I am feeling a little better, now."

"You had a very serious accident, Helga," Jeannie said with anxious concern on her face. "Are you sure you don't have any broken bones?"

"Mutter and Little Fawn looked me over real good," Helga said. "I don't hurt anywhere. I can move and do everything I should be able to do. But poor Morning Star, my poor Morning Star, what will happen to him?" Helga's tears fell again, and she dabbed at her eyes with her handkerchief.

Jeannie touched her best friend's face gently and looked her in the eyes. "Helga, I love Morning Star, too. But you know what must happen to animals when they hurt themselves badly." Jeannie tried to speak calmly. "And from what you say, Morning Star can't walk."

"Oh, Jeannie," Helga sobbed again. "I don't think I can bear two losses."

"God will give you the strength, Helga," Jeannie whispered. Her heart was aching for her friend. "I know He will. He's helping me go on without Pa. He knows your sadness. You can lean on Him." With a gentle hand, she brushed Helga's tangled hair away from her face.

"Billy Joe and I will always be here for you," Jeannie said, giving Helga a reassuring kiss on her forehead.

"Billy Joe will be so disappointed," Helga murmured.

"Yes, I'm sure he will be, Helga, but he'll be more concerned about you," Jeannie said. Making her voice sound cheerful, she continued, "Try and think on this—as long as you're recovering all right, you and Billy Joe can have other children in the future."

"Ja, I hope so," Helga said softly. "But I'll never forget what happened today." Her voice caught on another sob. "I wanted the baby so much."

"Helga, it might help you to know, I believe, Pa in heaven will take care of the baby for you," Jeannie said.

"Do you really think so?"

"Yes," Jeannie said, nodding her head firmly. "Pa's awful good with little critters and babies. He'll take good care of your baby."

Helga sighed. "Thank you, Jeannie," she said. "That makes me feel better. Thank you for telling me that. What would I do without you, my best friend?" Then Helga yawned and murmured, "I think that Little Fawn's medicine has made me sleepy."

"Good, Helga. Close your eyes and rest."

Henry stepped in the doorway and nodded to Jeannie. "I'll be right back, dear. Try and sleep," Jeannie said.

When Jeannie closed the bedroom door, Henry whispered, "I had to shoot Morning Star."

Jeannie slumped against the bedroom wall; and holding her head in her hands, let the silent tears fall. Diamond's first little son was dead. So many childhood memories of happy times raced through her thoughts. She remembered Helga riding Morning Star and she riding Diamond, two friends on their special mounts, riding together and enjoying the sweet smelling prairie grass dotted with acres and acres of colorful wildflowers.

"He was too far-gone, Shorty," Henry said in a voice heavy with frustration. "Morning Star could never walk again. There was just nothing else I could do." His shoulders slumped and he shrugged helplessly.

Jeannie nodded. "I know, Henry. I expected as much." She patted her brother's shoulders. Then she took a deep breath and straightened again. "I'll tell her myself," she said. "I'll tell her in awhile—when she's a little more rested."

Chapter 11
"Jack Comes to Visit"

"Look, Junior," Jeannie said, sweeping the front porch steps. She paused and peered down the path leading to her house. "Who could that be riding up the trail?" Junior perked up his ears and wagged his tail in a friendly way.

"Now I see who it is," Jeannie said. "It's Jack."

Jack pulled his horse to a stop at the hitching rail. "Morning, Miss Jeannie," he said, doffing his hat and dismounting.

"Good morning, yourself," Jeannie said, smiling a warm welcome. "Come inside, and I'll pour you a glass of buttermilk."

"Sounds inviting," Jack said, leaning down to pat Junior. Then he followed Jeannie into the kitchen.

"Sit down and I'll get us some cookies." Jeannie put her broom in the kitchen closet. Carrying buttermilk, cookies, and glasses to the table; she seated herself across from Jack, poured buttermilk, and offered him cookies.

"Thanks," he said taking a bite of oatmeal cookie and a drink of buttermilk. "Hmm! This cookie tastes good," he said.

"Glad you like it," Jeannie said, smiling. "How have you been, Jack? I haven't seen you in a month or so. How's the farm doing?"

"It's thriving," Jack said. "That's why I'm here."

"Oh?" Jeannie said, with a puzzled expression.

"Yes, ma'am," Jack said. "Pa signed his land over to me. The other day he said he's reached the age where he'd like to sit on the front porch in his rocking chair and whittle on a piece of cedar wood with his pocketknife."

Jeannie chuckled and said, "I've had that same kind of feeling, myself."

"Our cotton is doing fine," Jack's voice was enthusiastic. "We've got a new crop of peanuts planted, too. We hear tell that it'll be a good selling crop in the future. Lots of folks are giving over their acreage to peanuts."

"Yes, and some folks are planting orchards of peaches," Jeannie added. "It seems the farmland around here is good for growing them."

Jack impulsively reached across the table for Jeannie's hands and leaned in closer. "I guess you know," he said, trying to speak calmly, "I've been waiting a long time to get up the nerve to come over and share my feelings with you."

Jeannie felt a knot in her stomach. What was Jack going to say to her? Was she ready to hear it?

Jack took a deep breath and looked at her with fondness in his gaze. "Jeannie, girl, I'm asking you to marry me," he said in a shaky voice. "I've been loving you for a long time, ever since we were kids when me and my brother Billy Joe and Helga and you went fishing together in the Leon River."

"I remember," Jeannie said softly, lowering her eyes. "That was a happy time."

Jack nodded. With a look of anxious expectancy, he waited for her reply.

Jeannie raised her face. "Jack, I'm proud—mighty proud—that you have feelings for me," she said slowly, meeting his gaze, "and, I do hope you'll understand—when I say that I'm not ready for marriage now. I don't have my thoughts anywhere near such a thing."

Jack withdrew his hands and straightened. Disappointment clouded his hazel eyes.

"Grannies! I have so much to do here on the ranch." Jeannie rushed on quickly, "This year there's a lot of new colts, and I'm trying to add to the stock I already have, and I've been looking for buyers from back East—"

"Well, I reckon, Slim is a big help to you," Jack interrupted. "He could take over for you."

"Yes, he is a good help," Jeannie agreed, "but I'm not ready to leave all my ranching duties to him."

After a few painful moments of silence, Jack rose and reached for his hat. "Well, then," he said coolly, "I guess there isn't much more for me to say here." There was hurt in his voice, and he struggled to overcome his disappointment.

"Jack," Jeannie said, touching his arm gently, "I'm so sorry. I'd still like to be your friend."

Jack nodded stiffly and turned to leave. "I'd best get back to my farm duties," he said tersely. "Thanks for the buttermilk and cookies."

"Jack, don't hurry off," Jeannie said, following his quick strides. She was at a loss as to what to say to him. She heard the hard sound of his boots striking the parlor floor, and the sound of his spurs jingled loudly in her ears. Reaching the front porch together, she said, "Please, Jack—please, don't go away mad."

Despite all her efforts to make him understand her reasons for not accepting his proposal of marriage, Jeannie could feel Jack's anger. She touched the circular porch post and watched him mount. Saying nothing, he put his finger politely to the brim of his hat, but he didn't look at her. With a quick jab, he set his spurs to his horse and raced back down the trail, leaving a little cloud of dust to settle in the yard.

Weakly, Jeannie collapsed in the porch swing and tried to review Jack's brief visit. Could she have been less blunt? Could she have explained her feelings more gently? Her happy mood of a few minutes ago had suddenly turned to black gloom. The rest of the hot, August day ahead would be long, and her thoughts would be troubled.

Jeannie sighed and fought back tears of frustration. She hadn't wanted to hurt Jack. She liked him as a friend, but she honestly didn't have any thoughts of marriage for him or for anyone else.

As she blinked and wiped her tear-filled eyes on her apron, she caught sight of Slim strolling up from the barn. How she needed someone to talk to! Slim had always been a good listener when she shared her ranch plans and problems. Could he help her think through what had just happened?

"Morning, Little Lady," Slim said. "Did I see Jack riding away on his horse faster than a jackrabbit being chased by Junior?"

Jeannie smiled in spite of herself. "Yep, he was madder than a wet hen," she said teary-eyed.

Slim plopped down on the porch steps and stretched out his long legs. "Is that so? Want to talk about it?"

Jeannie nodded and took a deep breath. Feeling her face redden with embarrassment, she looked down at her hands in her lap and began slowly, "Well, Jack proposed to me—and, I guess what it amounted to, was that I told him no, even though, I tried to be careful in choosing my words."

"I reckon, he took it hard," Slim said, pursing his lips thoughtfully. "Jack's a mighty proud man."

Jeannie nodded again. "I tried to explain about the ranch and how busy I am."

Slim sighed. "And you told him—you're not thinking about marriage to anyone," he added.

"Uh-huh," Jeannie said. "I reckon, you know that much about me."

"I do know that much, Little Lady," Slim said with a pensive look in his eyes.

"I didn't want to hurt him or make him mad," Jeannie explained. "So I just told him the truth." She sighed. "I guess I was a little blunt."

"Well, it's best to get it said," Slim commented. "No need to beat around the bush about something that serious. You did the right thing. I reckon, Jack will get over it."

"I hope so," Jeannie said, reaching for a loose strand of hair from her long braid. She twisted it nervously around her finger. "I'd still like to be friends, but I don't think he wants my friendship right now."

"Maybe you should just let some time go by," Slim suggested softly.

For a moment, Jeannie and her ranch foreman sat together in silence. Then Slim said lightly, "You sure do have a 'down in-the-mouth' look on your pretty little face."

Jeannie sighed. "I was just thinking about all the awful things that have happened this year. It makes me sad to think on them."

Slim nodded. "Well, Little Lady, I reckon it hasn't been very easy for you," he said. He lifted his hat and ran his fingers through his sandy-colored hair. Junior lay beside him and nudged his nose against Slim's hand until Slim reached over and ruffled the dog's coat.

"I sure do miss Pa," Jeannie said. "He went so sudden-like."

"Uh-huh, he did," Slim agreed. "He was a mighty good man."

"Yes, he was," Jeannie said. "And poor Helga—she lost her baby. On top of that—Henry had to shoot Morning

Star, Diamond's first son." Jeannie felt her eyes filling with tears again.

"When troubles come, it shore seems like that old saying, 'when it rains it pours,' and that's a fact," Slim said, rubbing his chin thoughtfully. "But, try to look on the brighter side of things. You're young. You have a thriving ranch. Life can't stay bad forever. You're prospering, and things should be getting better for everyone." He gazed at Jeannie with a gentle smile.

"Many thanks for all those words of encouragement, Slim," Jeannie said smiling back and dabbing her eyes with her apron. "You've lifted my gloomy spirits already."

"Whoo-ee!" Slim exclaimed, removing his hat and fanning his face with it. "I know one thing for shore! I'm starting to burn up sitting out here in this hot sun." He took out his handkerchief and wiped his forehead. Then he stood and leaned an arm against the porch post. "I've been thinking," he said. "How would you like to ride up in the hills and see how your waterfall is doing this time of the year?"

"Oh, Slim, I would," Jeannie said, her voice brightening. "Let's go. This dress is too hot, and I feel like going for a swim. My overalls will be just fine for that."

Slim's face broke out in a wide grin. "All right, Little Lady," he said. "I'll saddle up Diamond, and you put on your old overalls, and we'll go riding to your special water pool. We'll jump right in and go swimming. That ought to cool us off some on this hot day!"

Chapter 12
"A Surprise Discovery"

"Slim, how did you know a cool swim was exactly what I needed on a humid and muggy day?" Jeannie asked, riding along beside Slim through the shady cedars and oaks on their return trip home from their swim in the water pool in the hills.

"I reckon, I'm just a mind-reader," Slim said, grinning. He reached over for a cedar twig and held it in his mouth like a toothpick, moving it from side to side, tasting its flavor.

"Well, I do feel a lot better," Jeannie said.

"You look a lot better, too," Slim said. "I mean—you don't have that sad look on your face, anymore. Course, you might have to re-comb that braid of yours," he said, grinning. He leaned over and gave it a little yank.

Jeannie was startled for a moment. He had done the same thing Pa had often done. So many other similar times flooded her memory—times when Pa had found a way to give her long braid a loving yank. She looked over at Slim and said, "Pa used to do that."

"I know. I reckon, I saw him do it, many a time," Slim said softly. He gave Miss Sunrise a little prod and trotted on ahead.

Jeannie touched her heels to Diamond's side and loped up beside Miss Sunrise. "So, now you're going to be acting like my pa?" Jeannie asked, with a grin.

"Nope," Slim said. "Just felt like doing it, is all."

Leaving the cedars, they crested a little hill and looked down into a small pool of black liquid. "Now, what could that be?" Slim asked, drawing closer to the pool. "I haven't seen that black pool before."

"I don't think we've ever ridden this way before," Jeannie said. "We are farther east today than we usually ride to get back home."

They reined in their horses at the pool's edge. Slim dismounted and knelt down beside the black liquid. With a finger he touched the liquid, then brought it to his nose, smelled it, and put a little dab on his tongue and tasted it.

Jeannie sat on Diamond, watching Slim's strange behavior. "What in the world are you doing?" she asked.

Slim didn't answer. He stood and reached in his shirt pocket and brought out a match. He struck his thumbnail across the match, bringing a flame. Then he dropped the burning match into the liquid and moved away quickly. Suddenly, the black pool burst into flames.

"Be careful, Slim!" Jeannie cried. "What's going on? The whole pool is burning!"

"It's oil!" Slim cried, slapping his hands against his leg. Grinning, he said, "You've got oil on your land."

"Oil?" Jeannie asked, puzzled.

"Yep, oil, Little Lady! You're gonna be rich!" Slim raised his hat and finger combed a few strands of sandy-colored hair away from his forehead.

"I don't know what you're talking about, Slim," Jeannie said, dismounting. She stood beside Slim and watched the burning pool of oil.

"Well, Little Lady, these days, oil is needed all over the world to run machines and to run that newfangled contraption they call the automobile. I saw a couple of automobiles in Ranger when I was in town last week. Automobiles will soon be driven by folks when they want to get somewhere," Slim said. "Pretty soon, horses and wagons and buggies will all be a thing of the past."

"Oh, I don't believe that," Jeannie said, amazed. "I don't want to ever get in an automobile. I saw a picture of one in a magazine, and they look scary to me. They go too fast! I think they can go at least ten miles an hour."

"I reckon, you've got some mighty hard thinking to do, Little Lady," Slim said in a somber voice. "If you drill for oil here on you land, you could become a very rich lady."

"But I don't want an oil well here," Jeannie protested. "I want my horse ranch. I want to breed and raise horses!"

"Well, you won't get rich just doing that alone," Slim argued. "Maybe you should think about all the things you could buy, and all the things you could do, with all the money you'll get from your oil well."

The oil puddle was burning out. Jeannie and Slim mounted and rode silently back to the house, deep in thought. It seemed to Jeannie, it was just one shock after another these days, and not all of them were welcomed! This new discovery was not a welcomed one, to her way of thinking. All these years, she'd had her hopes set on her horse ranch, and now, here came a decision she had to make about whether or not she wanted an oil well on her land.

That night Jeannie wrote about her frustrations in her journal:

Slim rode over and brought Henry and Ma back with him. He took Henry and showed him the oil puddle. Ma and I talked about what I should do. Ma said, if I went ahead and drilled for oil, and I had a successful well, then I could pay off my loan at the bank with the oil money. And there would probably be enough money to get up a good savings. With the savings, she said she didn't see any reason why I couldn't keep on raising my horses. So, I guess that's what I'll do. Slim says he knows some ranchers in Ranger who have also found oil on their land. It seems there's going to be an oil boom in this area. I wonder if I am ready for such a thing.

Chapter 13
"Slim's Surprise"

Three Years Later

"Well, Little Lady, it looks like I can't be your ranch foreman any longer," Slim said, sipping his cup of coffee at the kitchen table.

"Why is that?" Jeannie asked, reaching for the platter of eggs on the table. She put two eggs on her plate and a few slices of bacon.

"I've been keeping back a surprise from you," Slim said.

Jeannie wrinkled her brow. "Well, it's been nothing but surprises these past few years," she said wryly. "First, my well came through, and I found out I have a good-sized reserve of oil in the ground. I was happy about that. I remember you rode into town with me. I paid off my ranch mortgage and started up a sizeable savings account. Now, I'm having good luck selling my horses to buyers in the East. I even added some Texas longhorn cows last year after you fenced in part of the pasture for them, because I didn't want them mixing in with my horses."

Jeannie smiled, remembering the look of delight on Helga's face, when she told her she had so much oil money coming in, that for her birthday present, she was building her a schoolhouse.

Because Helga wanted the schoolhouse built on hers and Billy Joe's land, since the church could no longer be a school, Jeannie granted Helga's wish and had the school built on their property.

"Slim, ever since a wagon train of folks came to Ranger in 1880, folks have been settling here faster than fleas can hop on a hound dog," Jeannie said, buttering a biscuit.

"Yep, that's a fact." Slim nodded.

"And oil wells have been springing up all over. Mr. Markham has one, Ma and Henry have one, and now, even Helga and Billy Joe have an oil well," Jeannie said. "Why, just the other day, Helga told me her ma and pa were taking little Frankie with them on a trip to Germany pretty soon, so Mrs. Markham can visit her relatives back there."

"Uh-huh," Slim said, chewing on a bite of bacon. "And Eagle Feather is now Mr. Markham's foreman, and Waco is his top hand. Gray Wolf is practically all grown up now. He's a good enough hand to take over being your foreman."

"He's tall like his pa," Jeannie said. "He's shot up like a weed! He's a likeable young man, and he sure loves horses." She sipped her coffee. "But, Slim, why can't you keep on being my foreman?"

"Well, I guess I can't keep it a secret from you any longer, Little Lady," Slim said with a mischievous grin. "After we found that oil puddle on your land, a few years ago, I bought some land in Ranger with money I'd saved up. I was planning to raise longhorns on it. I reckon, you might have been wondering why I've been going to Ranger, at least once or twice a week, since then."

"Yes, you sure have been busy these past three years running back and forth into the city," Jeannie said.

"That's because I have three pumping oil wells on my land, and there could be several more coming in the future. That's why I can't be a good ranch foreman for you anymore."

"Why, Slim!" Jeannie exclaimed. "You sly ole fox! And all this time you've been working for me for fifty dollars a month, foreman's wages. I'm sure you have more money than I ever thought of having with all those pumping oil wells. I can't understand why you stayed on working for me?"

Slim gave her a friendly wink. "Why, Little Lady, I just wanted to help make sure your dream of running a successful horse ranch came true," he said, patting her hand. "I think it has. And yes, let's say I'm not hurting for much of anything. But the best part is I've built me a very nice house on the land. I think you'll like it. I want you come out and see it."

"Why, I'd love to see your house," Jeannie said, refilling Slim's coffee cup. "I'm sure it's a fancy one."

"Some folks think so," Slim said, smiling modestly as he stirred sugar in his coffee.

"And that fancy automobile you've been driving. All this time, I was thinking, you must owe the bank a passel of money," Jeannie teased. "Grannies! I was even beginning to worry that you were over-extending yourself. I'm sure it's yours, free and clear."

"It is," Slim said grinning. "I'm mighty glad you're not afraid to get in it and go riding to town to do your errands."

Jeannie breathed a heavy sigh. "It sure seems that more and more folks are driving automobiles these days," she said. "I reckon, I have to keep up with the times."

"You must admit, an automobile gets you where you want to go a lot faster than a horse and buggy," Slim said, finishing his coffee.

"Yes, but folks miss a lot riding—so fast. They don't get a chance to really enjoy the beauty of nature, the trees, and the pretty wildflowers growing all along the roadside," Jeannie said, rising and beginning to clear the table. "And someone is going to have to see that we get better roads. These wagon trails are all right for horses and buggies, but they sure are rough riding for folks in an automobile."

"That's another thing," Slim said. "I'm a member of the Citizen's Council in the cities near and around the Eastland and Ranger area. We've been thinking about improving the roads around here."

"Well, for goodness sakes!" Jeannie exclaimed with her hands on her hips. "Now, anything else, I don't know about you?"

"Oh, yes," Slim said, smiling mysteriously. "There's plenty. But you can learn all about me if you want to."

"How's that?" Jeannie asked.

Slim rose and stood beside her. He put his hands lightly on her waist and looked into her eyes. "Well, you can spend a lifetime with me, if you'd like," he said. "I've waited a long time for you, Little Lady. I'd like to marry you, if you'll have me."

"Why, Slim," Jeannie murmured shyly, lowering her head. Her face colored bright red with embarrassment. "I don't know what to say."

"Just say, 'yes'," Slim whispered. "I love you, Little Lady. I'll do everything I can to make you happy." He put a gentle finger under Jeannie's chin and lifted her face and kissed her.

"Oh, Slim," Jeannie whispered, as she caught her breath again. "I need some time to think about this."

"Take all the time you want, Little Lady," Slim said, giving her a peck on her forehead and a gentle yank on her braid. "I've waited a lot of years for you to grow up, ever since Mr. Markham and us boys helped you and your pa get his horses back from those Comanche rustlers. I reckon, I can wait awhile longer."

"I'm deeply touched, Slim," Jeannie said softly. "Have you really cared for me all this time?"

"I most certainly have. I'll admit to you, I couldn't have been happier, when you told me you refused Jack. I was afraid I'd lose you to him."

Jeannie smiled remembering. "Once Helga told me that you and Jack both had feelings for me, but I didn't really believe her." Jeannie returned to clearing the table.

"Well, Helga was right," Slim said, joining in and carrying his empty coffee cup to the kitchen cabinet counter. "I'm just glad Billy Joe introduced Jack to a nice girl who works in the bank with him. And I'm even more glad that Jack married her last year."

Jeannie smiled and doubled up her fist. She gave Slim a little poke on his arm while they stood at the kitchen counter together.

"I'm happy for them, too," Jeannie said, reaching for the teakettle on the stove. She poured hot water in a dishpan. "At last, I know Jack has no hurt feelings toward me. I like his wife, Betty Lou. She's a sweet girl."

Standing in the doorway, Slim put his black hat on his head. "I'll instruct Gray Wolf on what he should be doing, and then I'm going to drive back to Ranger," he said. "I don't want to be away from my oil wells too long. They're beginning to keep me mighty busy."

"Of course, Slim, I understand," Jeannie said.

"And I hope you'll say 'yes' to being my wife," Slim said with a gentle smile. "I know I won't be getting much shut-eye until I hear your answer."

"I promise, Slim," Jeannie said softly. "I'll be sure and give it some serious thought."

Slim nodded and politely touched a finger to his hat brim and left.

Chapter 14
"New Babies"

"Come, Diamond, ole boy," Jeannie said at Diamond's stall in the barn. "I'll saddle you up today. We're going to visit Helga and her new baby girl." Jeannie lifted the saddle Slim had given her for her sixteenth birthday and put it on Diamond's back.

"I guess some folks think I'm too soft to know how to saddle up my own mount these days, right boy? You are getting pretty old, I'll agree, but you've fathered some nice little colts this year. And we're going to take one of your sons, who looks just like you, and give him to Helga."

Just then Gray Wolf entered the barn holding the halter rope of a little black colt with a diamond-shaped tuft of hair in the middle of his forehead—in the exact same place as the one belonging to his father. "Tie him to the stall there," Jeannie said. "And you saddle up and go with me. I want you to bring the little colt with us. We'll be taking him to Helga."

"Yes, ma'am," Gray Wolf said. "She will like him. He looks much like Morning Star."

"Yes, he does," Jeannie agreed.

"Your sister, Prairie Flower, is such a good help. She is going to make a peach cobbler pie for you and me. When we get back home we'll have us some buttermilk and pie," Jeannie said.

"I like cobbler pie," Gray Wolf said, mounting his horse. When he saw Junior moving in to stand beside Jeannie and Diamond, he jerked his horse's reins, pulling him aside and called a warning, "Stay away from Swift Horse's hooves, Junior. He might kick you."

"Stay by me, Junior," Jeannie said, riding Diamond out of the barn. "When we get to Ma's place you can stop off and play with your sister, Princess, and little Matthew's dog, Belle. I'll be back for you after I finish visiting with Helga."

Junior looked up and wagged his tail as if he understood Jeannie's words as he trotted beside Diamond. Gray Wolf and the little colt followed behind.

When they arrived, Helga was sitting in the porch swing holding her baby in her arms. Jeannie dismounted and hurried to the swing. "Is she asleep?" she asked in a low whisper.

Helga nodded and lifted the pink baby quilt from the infant's face.

"Oh," Jeannie murmured, "she's so beautiful! And she's going to have cotton-white hair just like yours." She touched the fine, white curls on the baby's head. "Is she sleeping good at night?"

Helga's face glowed with happiness. She smiled and said, "Lorri is such a good baby. She seldom cries, and she's always smiling. Little Billy Joe Jr. was a bit more troublesome, and he didn't sleep well, because he often had the colic."

"Where is he?" Jeannie asked, looking about.

"He's inside taking a nap. He is such an active two-year-old." Helga gave a little sigh. "He's into everything now. I have to keep my eyes on him all the time."

"Well, his father is Billy Joe," Jeannie said, with a knowing grin. "What do you expect? Remember what a tease he was?"

"Ja, I do," Helga said smiling. "But I thank God every day for my two wonderful children."

"I know you love them dearly," Jeannie said. "They are both precious. I am so happy for you and Billy Joe and your little family."

Gray Wolf dismounted and stood at the hitching rail. He held the little colt's halter rope.

"Hello, Gray Wolf," Helga called.

"Howdy, ma'am," Gray Wolf said politely.

"Helga, we brought Diamond's little son for you. Maybe, someday, when little Billy Joe Jr. is older, he can ride him," Jeannie said.

"Oh, Jeannie," Helga exclaimed, handing her baby daughter to her friend. She walked to the porch steps and Jeannie followed. "He is adorable," Helga squealed. "He looks just like Morning Star when he was a colt." She stepped down to inspect the little horse. She touched his face and put her arms around his neck. "I love him," she said. Tears of gratitude glistened in her eyes. "Thank you so much, Jeannie."

"Gray Wolf, please take him down to the pasture gate and let the little fellow inside the pasture to graze," Jeannie said. "And it would be helpful if you could chop some extra wood for Helga's wood bin when you return."

"Yes, ma'am, I will," Gray Wolf said.

"Thank you, Gray Wolf. I could use some more wood for the stove," Helga said, stepping back on the porch. "You are so thoughtful, Jeannie." Helga put her arm around her friend's waist, and the two young women returned to the swing and seated themselves.

"It's Easter vacation, and the children aren't in school," Helga said. "I think this is such a beautiful time of the year. Look at all those lovely wildflowers growing everywhere, as far as the eye can see."

Jeannie looked to the pasture and to the fields beyond. "They are mighty pretty," she said. "And there's babies everywhere, too. I have baby colts and baby calves, and you have two beautiful babies."

"Ja, that's true. You know, Jeannie, I think it is time you think of such things for yourself. I am wondering, whether you will ever know the joy of holding your very own little baby in your arms, just as you are holding my little Lorri."

"Well, that's part of the reason why I'm here, Helga," Jeannie said, turning to look at her friend. "Several days ago Slim asked me to marry him. He's in Ranger at his ranch waiting for my answer."

"There! Didn't I tell you he had feelings for you years ago?" Helga said with a satisfied nod. "He has been waiting a long time for you."

"That's what he told me," Jeannie said. "I really didn't believe it all these years, but I guess you were right about that, after all."

Helga smiled and said, "Jeannie, I remember when we were younger, how you used to tell me you would never even consider getting married." Helga gave a little chuckle. "You were always too busy thinking about getting your horse ranch someday."

"I remember," Jeannie said.

"So what is to stop you now?" Helga asked with a slight tone of exasperation in her voice. "You are rich. And Slim is even richer. We had to keep his secret success from you, because he wanted to tell you himself. It wasn't easy, but Billy Joe and I did it."

The baby began to wiggle and squirm around in Jeannie's arms. With a little whimper she began to suck on her fist. Jeannie rocked her a little from side to side. "You knew about Slim's oil wells all along?" Jeannie asked.

"Ja," Helga said nodding her head. She reached for little Lorri. "You have been so busy with your horses, you haven't had time to know what is going on in Ranger. It is becoming a booming oil town these past few months." Shifting Lorri to her bosom, Helga made preparations to nurse the infant.

"I reckon the town is really growing fast," Jeannie said thoughtfully.

"It is," Helga said. "Ranger is filled with people, hoping to strike it rich in the oil boom."

Jeannie frowned. "I don't know whether I will like that too much," she said. "I'm mighty glad my land isn't all filled up with oil wells."

Helga smiled and looked at her friend. "You're a special girl, Jeannie," she said. "You deeply love nature and the outdoors, don't you?"

Jeannie nodded. "I do, sure enough."

Helga gazed lovingly at her baby daughter, lying gently in her arms. She watched her little infant nurse and gently touched the baby's white curls along the crown of her head.

Jeannie was moved by the beauty of mother and child in their quiet harmony with one another. Was there something missing in her own life? Was it now time for her to experience the joy of being a wife and mother? Was it now time to know the sort of happiness and contentment Helga expressed?

Helga lifted her gaze, as if reading her friend's thoughts, and said, "Jeannie, you and I have been best friends ever since I came from Germany and you taught me my first words in English."

"That's a fact," Jeannie said, smiling.

"Well, I will tell you after all our years together, and because you are my best friend, now and always—I think it is time for you to be married." Helga's eyes held a look of concern. "Your ranch is successful. It isn't good for you to live alone. You are rich and Slim loves you, and you know he would make a wonderful husband."

"Maybe someday," Jeannie said slowly. "This is all so sudden for me."

"Ja, well, it's not sudden for Slim," Helga reminded, somewhat impatiently. "I don't want to sound like I am lecturing you, but I worry about you, Jeannie, dear. I am so happy with Billy Joe and our children. I want you to know the same kind of joy I have. I don't want to see you become a lonely old maid." Helga paused, studying the serious expression on her friend's face. There was something new in Jeannie's eyes—something, she had never seen before.

"Well, anyway, I'm happy to see you are finally giving marriage some thought," Helga said in a lighter tone.

Jeannie shook her head and chuckled. "Yes, Helga, I am. For the first time, I really am," she said, hugging her friend. "And if I marry anyone, it will be Slim. Does that make you feel a little better?"

"Ja, it does," Helga said with a happy smile. She put little Lorri over her shoulder and gently patted her back until she heard a tiny burp. "But I don't think you should wait, Jeannie. It might not be long before someone in Ranger will see what a good man Slim is and take him away from you."

Jeannie considered Helga's warning. Although Helga was smiling, Jeannie could see she was sincere about what she had said. The two friends rocked together in the swing in silent companionship, as they had often done in their growing up years. Jeannie leaned her head against the back of the swing, wondering how she would feel if someone else married Slim. Grannies! What would she do? She had grown to depend on him so much these past years. They could talk about most anything. He had become her close friend—almost as close as Helga.

What would she do if he were no longer in her life? The thought was troubling. She remembered the strange pounding of her heart when he kissed her. Why did she feel so comfortable in his arms? Just thinking about him made her feel breathless and her heart was beginning to beat faster.

Maybe—she shouldn't wait too long. Maybe—she should hitch up the buggy and ride over to Slim's ranch in Ranger and give him her consent. Maybe—she would do that first thing in the morning.

"Helga," Jeannie said softly. "I'm going into Ranger tomorrow."

"To say 'Ja,' I hope. Will it be, Ja?" Helga asked, smiling brightly.

"Yes, it will be 'Ja,' Helga," Jeannie said, with a happy giggle. "And you will be my maid of honor, just as I was your maid of honor at your wedding."

"Oh, Jeannie!" Helga cried, giving her friend a warm hug with her free arm. "I love weddings! I can't wait to help you with your wedding. Why don't you go find Slim right now and tell him 'yes,' today? Then we can begin to plan your wedding."

"Hmm!" Jeannie considered that happy thought. "Maybe I should tell him today," she said grinning, catching Helga's enthusiasm. "Maybe I should. Oh, grannies! I think I'll go right now!" She sprang out of the swing, hurried down the porch steps, and took Diamond's reins and mounted.

"Tell Gray Wolf I'm riding Diamond to Ranger. And tell him to ask Prairie Flower to save me a piece of her peach cobbler pie!"

"I will," Helga said, giggling happily as she watched her friend move into quick action. She shifted little Lorri to her shoulder and waved goodbye. "I'm so excited for you, Jeannie. I'll be on pins and needles until I see you again."

"Goodbye, Helga," Jeannie said, turning Diamond down the trail. "I'll be seeing you soon."

Approaching the house where she had grown up with Ma and Pa and Henry, Jeannie halted Diamond in the meadow for a moment and gathered a bouquet of wildflowers. Then she rode to the graveyard nestled among the cedars and stepped over the little, white fence surrounding the two graves.

She knelt on the ground between the graves and put a bouquet on each grave. "Howdy, Pa," she said. "Howdy, Ole Blue. Reckon you both know why I'm here." She took a deep breath and said, "Yep, I reckon I'm gonna tie the knot with Slim. What do you think, Pa?"

Jeannie patted her father's grave. She felt a warm contentment as a soft, gentle breeze blew across her face. It was almost like Pa was tugging on her braid. "So, you think he's a good man? Well, I do too, Pa," Jeannie said. "I just wanted to let you know, I'll be a married lady soon. And Slim yanks on my braid, just like you used to do. I expect, you put that idea in his head," Jeannie said with a little smile playing at her lips.

Then she turned to her dear pet's grave. "Ole Blue, your children have pups scattered all over this countryside. I reckon you are related to most every hound dog hereabouts, and I sure am glad to have Junior with me. I reckon you know that, too. He's been mighty good company for me on my ranch, and he loves Slim. So I guess that suits you fine. Of course, Diamond is still with me. He's been daddy to a lot of nice colts these past few years. But one of these days, I'll have to let him roam around in the pasture and not do much of anything. He's been a faithful friend, just like you were, Ole Blue."

Rising, Jeannie stood beside the graves and said, "Well, I'll be going on into Ranger to tell Slim I'll be hitching up with him. I'd better do it now, before some city girl takes a liking to him and turns his head—like Helga said." Jeannie chuckled. "I don't think that would happen. But I don't want to take a chance on it."

In the oak tree nearby, a little brown squirrel fixed his eyes on Jeannie and began chattering. "Is that a fact?" Jeannie said.

She looked down on the two graves of her loved ones and gave each an affectionate pat. Then she rose. "Well, Pa and Ole Blue, Little Squirrel has just told me I'd better be on my way and go tell Slim I'll be his bride," she said. "I'll be visiting you again soon. I promise."

Jeannie stepped back over the fence and mounted Diamond. "Come on, boy," she said. "Let's ride to Ranger and find Slim."

Dear Friends of Jeannie, Helga, Henry, Billy Joe and all the other Texas folks,

I hope you enjoyed reading *Jeannie, A Texas Frontier Girl, Book Four*. For your special collection, you can purchase Books One, Two and Three, from Publish America by calling 240.529.1031 or purchase from their Internet site: http://www.publishamerica.com or any Internet book store: http://www.Amazon.com, http://www.barnesandnoble.com, http://www.walmart.com, and other Internet stores. You can also find the Jeannie series of books at your favorite bookstore, and you can ask for them at your local library. If you would like to chat with me, I will be happy to reply. My web page address:

http://www.authorsden.com/evelynhoran
Email: evelynhoran@aol.com.

And, since I am a grandma, I am sending BIG HUGS to all of you.

Happy Reading!   ☺   ☺   ☺

Evelyn Horan – Author
Jeannie, A Texas Frontier Girl, Books One, Two, Three, Four.